Titanic
A Ship Out of Time

Ashley Bristow

Titanic: A Ship Out of Time
Copyright © Ashley Bristow, 2013

ISBN-13: 978-1492732044
ISBN-10: 1492732044

One

They called it the unsinkable ship.

I was standing in front of the first class gangplanks, looking up at the *Titanic*. The massive black hull stretched into the harbor, further than I could see. The grainy photographs in the London newspapers hadn't done it justice.

She had never sailed before, but they already called the *Titanic* the grandest ship in the world.

Behind me was the coach that chauffeured my family to the port of Southampton. Out came my stepfather, Charles, and his servant, Mr. Rathbone. Rathbone took my mother's gloved hand as she stepped from the carriage, being careful not to trip over her long skirts.

"Oh, my word!" Mother exclaimed, her eyes scanning the height of the towering smokestacks. For the first time that morning, a genuine smile spread across her face.

She turned to my stepfather. "What a splendid way to travel home, Charles," she said, beaming.

"Only the best for you, Victoria," Charles replied.

But there was a hint of irritation in his voice.

He snapped his fingers, motioning for Mr. Rathbone to bring our pile of luggage forward. "Let's move along," he said. "I can't be the last gentleman aboard the ship."

Mother's face sagged as she stepped onto the dock. She'd fallen gravely ill six weeks ago and still moved slowly, but my stepfather was none the more patient for it. The owner of the Lake Erie Steel Company was going to make an entrance.

I watched Charles order the *Titanic*'s bellhops around, hovering over them as they loaded the luggage onto White Star Line carts.

"Careful with that one!" he barked. "There are valuables in there. I won't have anything broken when we dock. And put this one on top!"

"Yes, sir," the bellhop replied with a nervous smile.

Next out of the coach was the British nurse, Celia, holding my sister Sadie. At that moment, the *Titanic*'s funnels let off an enormous boom, strong enough to shake the ground beneath us. Sadie startled and pinned her hands over her ears.

"It's so loud!" she cried.

She had been cranky and disobedient ever since I arrived at Charles' and Mother's home in London. She fought relentlessly with Celia, responding to all the nurse's commands with a decisive *no*.

But today, I couldn't blame her. She was seven years old and as elegantly groomed as the grown-up women in the first class boarding area, donning her green satin dress and shiny black shoes. It had taken an hour to pin her hair against her scalp, transforming her straight dark hair into springy curls. She looked like a tiny version of Mother, prim and perfect.

Still, every time I looked at her, I pictured Celia and Mother stuffing her into petticoats and tugging her hair while she howled. She looked agitated even now, pulling at the brand new shoes.

"My toes hurt," she whined. "I want to take these shoes off."

I reached out and took her from the nurse's arms.

"Do you want to see the *Titanic*?" I asked her. "It's the biggest ship in the entire world."

She quickly shook her head no.

"Come on, Sadie. I bet you do," I said, and swung her over my shoulders, where she loved to sit. She let out a squeal of delight.

"Mommy, look!" she cried, her tiny finger pointing up toward the funnels.

Mother glared at me.

"John!" she hissed sharply. "Put her down and give her to Celia. Stop making a scene. And for heaven's sake, don't ruin her dress!"

Mother usually didn't mind when I played around with Sadie. But in this kind of company, she expected my sister to look like a china doll, with about as much spirit. And in any event, Charles frowned upon horseplay. He called it "unladylike."

We hadn't even boarded yet, and Charles' attitude was rubbing off on Mother. I vowed not to let it rub off on me, too.

"First class passengers, proceed to the gangplanks!" a crewman bellowed out, and the crowd began to inch forward. We worked our way towards the gangway doors with a throng of passengers dressed in their finest, butlers and maids trailing behind.

"John, take your ticket," Mr. Rathbone said, scowling as he thrust it at me. "I'm not going to hold it for you."

I knew my stepfather's servant didn't like me very much, and the feeling was mutual. I'd hoped Charles would dump Rathbone off in London and hire a new servant at home. Unfortunately, the crabby old man was coming to Cleveland, too.

I felt a rush of relief as I stepped from the gangway to the first class entrance of the *Titanic*.

Good riddance, England, I thought. *You won't be missed.*

We were greeted by stewards in crisp White Star Line uniforms, who smiled pleasantly and gave a little bow.

"Welcome aboard, Mr. Conkling!" one said. He looked us over with a generous smile. "I am Mr. Latimer, the head steward on the *Titanic*. We've been anticipating your family's arrival."

For a moment, I was taken aback that the stewards already knew us. But then I remembered that Lake Erie Steel did business with White Star. Some of the steel in the ship's gigantic hull was purchased from Charles.

"Thank you," Charles responded in his polite but formal tone. "This is my wife, Victoria, our daughter Sadie, and this…"

Charles always hesitated when he introduced me.

"This is John…my son."

"Wonderful," Mr. Latimer replied as he handed Charles and I each a red flower for the buttonholes in our jackets. "Mr. Bowen will show you to your staterooms."

A slight, balding man appeared, offering a handshake to Charles. "Come with me, please," he said chipperly. "I'll show you to your cabins on B-Deck."

We followed Mr. Bowen through the first class dining room, which was already set for dinner that night. Sun streaming through the portholes made the china sparkle. There were still creases in the stiff, brand-new tablecloths.

For the first time, I felt a twinge of excitement about being aboard the *Titanic*.

"The ship will be launching soon," Mr. Bowen said to me as I unpacked my suitcases. "You might want to go out on deck and see it.

There's a crowd gathering on the dock to wish us bon voyage. It's quite a sight!"

I could hear Sadie whining one door over: "But I don't *want* to wear this dress all day!"

I turned back to Mr. Bowen. "Yes, I think I will," I replied. "And I'll take my sister."

I poked my head into the adjacent stateroom, pretending to be oblivious to Sadie's mood.

"Sadie, do you want to go out on the Boat Deck with me?" I asked. "They'll be launching the ship soon, and we can wave to all the people. It'll be fun!"

Sadie's usually sad little face lit up at the mention of the word *fun*. Lord knew she hadn't had any lately, especially in London.

"Mommy, I want to go," she said.

"No, Sadie," Mother replied. "It's time to rest now. Celia will fix you some tea."

"No."

"Maybe it's time for a nap, then."

"*No*," she insisted, kicking her shiny black shoes. "I want to go!"

Charles cringed. Celia sucked in her breath, bracing herself for another tantrum.

"I'll take her," I offered again.

Mother frowned. "I don't know if it's..."

"She doesn't have to spend every minute with Celia, you know," I said. "We'll come back as soon as the ship pulls away."

"Fair enough," Charles replied before Mother could object. He waved his hand, as if he were eager to be rid of us.

*   *   *

The deck was crowded with passengers who pushed against the railing, marveling at the distance to the water. The *Titanic* had a height of more than seventy feet. Dock workers scurried around, preparing for the launch.

From our high perch, I could see where the *Titanic* sloped off to the lower decks at the stern. Another swarm of passengers had gathered there. I held Sadie around the waist and settled her against the rail, where she could watch the excitement on the docks. Another long, sonorous boom echoed from the funnels.

"Johnny, look!" She said, pointing. Her eyes were wide.

I tried to follow the aim of her outstretched finger. She was pointing down at the lower deck, where a single gull swooped down from time to time, hovering over the commotion.

"Bridie," Sadie said.

She was still little enough to mix up words in ways I couldn't always understand. I thought for a moment before it dawned on me.

"Oh, yes. It's a *birdie*," I said. "That's a seagull, Sadie. Do you remember the gulls on Lake Erie? I helped you feed them last year when we went to the beach."

My mind wandered back to the big house in Cleveland, on Euclid Avenue. Our street was known around the city as "Millionaire's Row." The house was lonely by now. Since I'd left for London, it had been abandoned for weeks. I thought back to the day I locked it up: the rows of windows shuttered, the magnificent flower garden dead and buried under a foot of snow. That day, I didn't know when I'd be back — or if Mother ever would.

Sadie looked back at me with glaring brown eyes, impatient with my dim-wittedness. I'd seen that same look on my mother's face thousands of times…at least, before she married Charles.

"*No*," she insisted. She leaned forward to peer over the railing, so far I nearly lost my grip. "Bridie."

I sighed.

"Bridie it is, then." I'd learned not to fight these battles, especially not with a seven-year-old who'd spent the morning being primped to look like a child mannequin in a department store window.

I looked over the railing at the other group of passengers. This group was far different from the lively, overdressed first class passengers who had arrived in Southampton by private coach, burying the bellhops with mountains of luggage. Their dress was drab.

Third class, I suddenly realized. They were immigrants, nearly all of them, who were leaving behind their lands and their families.

Soon enough, the *Titanic*'s doors slammed shut and the gangways were sealed off. With a great whir, the engines started for the very first time. I felt a shudder beneath my feet as the ship began to inch forward.

"Goodbye!" some of the passengers around me began to call to no one in particular. They were caught up in the excitement. Sadie waved, too.

The *Titanic* sailed faster now, moving majestically down the narrow channel. She towered over the tugboats as she glided past.

All of a sudden there were several loud snaps in a row, as loud as a hundred rifles firing at once. A gasp rose from the Boat Deck.

I pressed forward to see what was happening. Sadie clung to my jacket.

The passengers shrunk back in horror. The immense force of the *Titanic* had caused another ship's moors to snap, and the smaller ship glided directly toward us, as if it were being pulled by a magnet. The crowd's cheers and smiles gave way to screams as the ship drew closer.

"It's suction!" someone shouted.

The voices blurred together until I heard someone yell, "We're gonna hit!"

Just then the *Titanic*'s engines fired, and she gunned ahead. The suction broke. The second ship stopped moving, rocking helplessly in the channel. Its broken moors still floated on the surface of the water.

There was a collective sigh of relief. I felt Sadie's grip loosen.

"That was a close one," a man behind us said. "That ship nearly took out our stern."

"Yeah," replied another. "Let's hope it's not an omen."

Two

The first class staterooms were beautiful, but above all, I was grateful to have one to myself. Charles' and Mother's room was across the hall, and next to their room was Celia and Sadie's. Rathbone was stashed away somewhere on D-Deck. I hoped he'd stay down there for the remainder of the voyage, but I wasn't counting on it.

It had been a nightmarish month in London. I received the telegram one snowy day in March as I was holed up in my room at Oberlin College. I was studying for a Latin exam when I heard a knock on my door.

"We've bad news, Mr. Conkling," they said as they handed me the message.

Mother had collapsed, convulsing violently, and then fell into a coma for days. The doctors were baffled by her condition. I had to get there, and quickly—there might not be much time.

I boarded the ship to England prepared for another funeral. It had been ten years since my father died suddenly.

But by some stroke of luck, Mother was awake in her bed when I arrived. I held her hand as the nurses fussed over her. At first I was afraid she wouldn't recognize me, but as I leaned over her, she smiled.

"My Johnny's here," she told the nurses.

My eyes still stung a little at the thought of it. After my father died, she was the only person who still called me that.

Several days later, Charles announced we were going back to Cleveland in April. The doctor tried to reason with him, warning against taking Mother so soon. She'd be better off recovering fully in London, he said. A transatlantic crossing was too much for her, especially with Sadie in tow.

Charles would hear none of it.

"I have a business to run, damn it," he snapped. "I'll bring Sadie's nurse to take the burden off Victoria. Besides, she isn't happy in London. She's done nothing but complain since we got here."

The doctor persisted. "But we have yet to determine the cause of her collapse, Mr. Conkling," he said.

Charles rolled his eyes.

"Hysteria, I suspect," he replied.

I knew what people said about Mother. I'd heard the hushed chatter at society gatherings when they thought I wasn't listening: Victoria Conkling was "not well," as they politely called it, emotionally more so than physically. It was clear that Charles believed it, too.

Tension built inside the London house. Sadie threw fits. Mother still lay in bed all day. Charles brooded, pacing around the first floor in the middle of the night. He spent hours poring over documents from Lake Erie Steel.

They'd be my documents someday soon. Having no sons of his own, Charles had officially named me his successor.

At least inheriting the steel mills would make fodder for idle chatter at dinner tonight. Some of the wealthiest members of British and American society would be there, and I knew what to expect.

I stood before the mirror, examining myself. I had Mother's dark, straight hair and brown eyes, but other than that, I took after my father in every way.

I frowned into the mirror and hoped no one would comment on my lack of resemblance to Charles.

*   *   *

The *Titanic* was docked off the coast of France that evening, taking on passengers from the port of Cherbourg. I took the first class elevator toward D-Deck by myself, not caring to wait for Mother and Charles. There was tension between them again.

I watched the passengers descend the first class stairs, wearing long silken evening gowns or top hats. I recognized some of them as they entered the reception room. There was the elderly Straus couple, the owners of Macy's department store in New York. There was John Jacob Astor, the richest man aboard. He had his newest wife along for the voyage. According to gossip, Astor's first wife had gotten tired of his philandering and divorced him, and he and the new woman fled the States to avoid the publicity.

"What scandal!" one of the ladies had exclaimed gleefully at a party several months ago. "And to think he took up with a girl barely John's age. If I were Astor I'd hide out at the pyramids, too."

Egypt was the latest fashionable holiday destination for the rich. Always wanting to keep up, Mother had begged Charles to take her just a month before she collapsed.

"The pyramids are no place for you," he'd replied dismissively. "Come on now. You wouldn't be able to take the heat, not to mention the sandstorms and the lepers."

A few minutes later, my family arrived for dinner. Rather than looking irritated as he was this morning, Charles was cool and collected, nodding and greeting acquaintances as they passed. Sadie was sullen, clasping her favorite doll in her hand. Her other hand tugged at the giant bow perched atop her curls.

Mother was wearing the necklace.

The passengers who kept up with their gossip knew that Victoria Conkling's diamond necklace was the most valuable piece of jewelry on board. Charles had given it to her when they married eight years ago. Now the heavy cascade of diamonds rested around her neck, a striking contrast to her dark hair and pale skin.

My mind flashed to the stream of third class passengers I watched coming aboard this morning. That necklace was probably worth more than all of their belongings put together.

"John, I have someone I'd like you to meet," Charles said. Beside him stood a tall, olive-skinned man, his black hair slicked back against scalp. His features were sharp.

I knew who he was before Charles spoke.

"This is my friend, Mr. Gregory."

The dark-haired man extended his hand.

"Anton Gregory, of Gregory Galleries," he said. "It's a pleasure to finally meet Charles' boy." He scanned me up and down as he said it.

Anton Gregory *was* a gallery owner, and a rich one at that. But I'd heard the rumors that swirled through London society: he smuggled expensive pieces of art and jewelry back and forth across the Atlantic, from London to New York. He was foreign on his mother's side—Serbian, Charles said. He was also a notorious playboy.

I couldn't for the life of me understand Charles' friendship with this swarthy half-Englishman.

"It's nice to meet you, too," I replied, careful not to let my tone betray my thoughts.

"Let's sit down, shall we?" Charles said.

At the entrance to the dining saloon, Captain Edward Smith greeted his passengers with a gentlemanly smile. They called him the millionaire's captain. I knew some of the aristocrats aboard took special care to book trips with him. This voyage, however, would be the Captain's last. He was due to retire from the White Star Line after the *Titanic*'s maiden voyage ended in New York.

"I hope you enjoy your stay on the ship, Mr. Conkling," Smith said to Charles. "It's a pleasure to have you aboard."

"The pleasure is all mine, Captain."

Captain Smith turned to me. "And is this your son?" he asked.

"Yes," Charles replied without missing a beat. "My boy, John."

"I see your mother in you," Captain Smith said as he shook my hand.

I breathed a small sigh of relief that he said nothing comparing my appearance to Charles'.

Mother leaned in to me as we sat down to dinner. "Be sure to make conversation with Faye tonight," she said.

"And don't roll your eyes," she added, catching my expression before I could subdue it.

I'd forgotten Faye LaRoe and her mother would be on the ship. They were returning from a long trip to Europe after Mr. LaRoe passed away last summer. The LaRoes lived on Millionaire's Row in Cleveland, too. Mother was still harboring hopes that Faye and I would get married someday.

Not if I can help it, I thought, as Faye and Mrs. LaRoe sat down at our table. By the socialites' standards, she was perfect — ivory skin, blonde hair, impeccable posture. But her icy demeanor made her insufferable.

"Hi, Faye," I said.

"Hello," she replied without a smile.

Mrs. LaRoe was friendlier. "Good evening, John," she said. There was a man standing beside her, who looked slightly older than me — mid-twenties, maybe. "This is Max. He's offered to escort Faye and me during the voyage."

"Max Seligman," the man said, shaking my hand. "New York, New York. I'm a buyer for Macy's department store. And you're the steel tycoon, eh?"

"I'm a student," I replied.

"He's at Oberlin College for the time being," Charles interjected. "Once he tires of his schoolbooks, he'll be well-prepared to take over the business."

Our tablemates nodded approvingly. I knew Charles thought college was a waste of my time, and I suspected the others did, too.

"I'm studying Latin and foreign affairs," I said, hoping to break the awkward silence.

"Hey, speaking of foreign affairs," Max piped up, mercifully taking the focus away from me, "Mr. Gregory, I hear that you're a Serb."

"On my mother's side, yes," Anton replied.

"If you don't mind me asking, what do you think of the situation in the Balkans?" Max asked. His jaunty Brooklyn accent made the serious question sound like ordinary banter. "It sounds like a terrible mess."

There was a flash of anger in Anton's eyes.

"When Austria took Bosnia, Serbs were killed by the thousands," he said. "Serbia is enraged. Austria must know there will be hell to pay for such slaughter."

"However," he continued blithely, "I was born and raised in London. I pay little attention to such affairs."

I'd heard my professors talk about what they delicately called the "international situation." After Austria had seized Bosnia from the Turks four years ago, unrest was spreading throughout Europe — enough to cause a continent-wide war. I had trouble believing that Anton had no interest in what was brewing in his mother's homeland.

Anton turned his attention to Mother. "Mrs. Conkling, I hear you are still recovering from your illness. Please allow me to extend my sympathies."

Charles' face hardened. Mother's stiff posture slacked for a moment, and she shifted in her seat.

"Why, thank you, Anton," she said, looking down at her teacup.

"I trust you are feeling better?"

"Most of the time," she said.

Anton had a little smirk on his face. Why was he pressing the issue? It was impudent. But for some reason, he seemed to enjoy making Mother uncomfortable.

Sadie suddenly pushed her plate away.

"I'm not hungry," she announced, folding her arms over her chest.

Mother tried to diffuse her. "Drink your tea, Sadie," she said, gently nudging the saucer towards her.

"No. I said I don't want it."

"Well, then, maybe it's time to go back to Celia," Mother replied.

"No, no, no, no!" Sadie began to yell, as other passengers threw glances in our direction. Faye glared.

Sadie kicked her shoe against the table, causing the china to clatter.

"Sadie, hush!" Mother said, her face beginning to turn red as the stares intensified.

"I hate Celia," Sadie said, ignoring Mother's cajoles completely. "I want Bridie."

Another tantrum was underway, and Mother was powerless to stop it.

"Bridie's not here. Remember?" Mother said, looking increasingly anxious. "She left us."

"She is too here!" Sadie replied. "I saw her!"

It was Charles' and Anton's turn to look shocked. They sat with their forks frozen in their hands, exchanging stunned expressions.

"Who is she talking about?" I hissed to mother. I had never heard that name before — not at home, and certainly not in the London house.

"Not now, John," she muttered, refusing to look at me.

"Victoria, have the steward take Sadie to the nurse," Charles commanded. "She can eat in her stateroom. I won't have her ruining everyone else's supper."

"But…" Mother began.

"Now!" he insisted. "These people didn't buy a first-class ticket to listen to this ruckus."

Sadie's wails grew louder as Mother scooped her up and complied with Charles' orders, delivering her to a dining room steward.

"I want Bridie!" Sadie's voice echoed through the dining saloon. The other passengers looked away, politely pretending they hadn't noticed anything.

As soon as the dishes were cleared and Charles wandered off again to mingle with the other passengers, I went back to my stateroom. After today's strange series of events, the last thing I wanted to do was sip cocktails and talk business with the men.

Something was bothering me, but I couldn't pinpoint what it was. Why was Mother so ashamed of being ill? Even the doctors in London had determined she had done nothing to cause it. Maybe the gossip had come around to her, and she'd heard the comments from the other women in first class even as they envied her necklace.

She's a hysteric, I imagined them whispering. *She nearly had a nervous breakdown a month ago. What a pity. Let's move along before she talks to us.*

My thoughts were interrupted by a knock on the stateroom door. It was Mr. Bowen, my steward.

"Good evening, Mr. Conkling," he said. "I have a message for you."

"What is it, Mr. Bowen?"

I thought of the last time I'd received a knock on my door from someone bearing a message. I hoped nothing had come of Sadie's tantrum, that it hadn't caused Mother another fit of anxiety.

"Your father would like you to meet him in the smoking room," he said. "It is on A-Deck, if you haven't yet been there."

I was taken aback. Not that Charles was in the smoking room, probably enjoying a third or fourth round of liquor, as he often did at night. It just wasn't like him to invite me along.

"Did he say why?" I asked.

"No, sir, he didn't. Perhaps he'd like you to join him for a game of blackjack," Mr. Bowen replied, smiling.

I put on my jacket and took the stairs to the smoking room, where the first class men retreated at night with cigars and stiff drinks. No women were allowed in there.

Charles was sitting at a table alone, his drink half-empty before him, another sitting at the table's empty seat. When he spotted me, the look on his face told me this meeting had a purpose—and it wasn't blackjack.

"Care for a brandy?" Charles asked as I slid into the seat.

I hated brandy, but Charles didn't know that. He had never once offered me a drink before.

"I'm sure you wondered why I asked to meet you here," Charles said.

"I thought maybe you needed a drink after Sadie's fit tonight," I replied. "She doesn't like her new nurse. Maybe in Cleveland we can find a new one."

Charles cut me off. "John, please, this isn't about the nurse," he said. "Something very serious is going on. Something that could ruin us…"

He paused and let the words the words sink in.

"…Ruin *you*."

"What is it?" I asked. "Mother? I know the doctors never did diagnose her."

"No, but it certainly won't help her condition," Charles replied. "You know she's not well, which is why I'm going to ask you not to discuss it with her. Do I make myself clear?"

I nodded.

"A former servant from our house in London has stolen a confidential document from me," Charles said. "One that could do immense damage to Lake Erie Steel's reputation, if it ever gets to the newspapers. The *Plain Dealer* would go to town with it."

"Do you know where it is?" I asked.

"Thanks to your sister, I do now," he replied. "I thought she was merely imagining things until I checked with the purser. It turns out the thief is on board."

I pieced the day's events together in my head. Sadie hadn't been mistaken when she stubbornly corrected me on the Boat Deck. Looking down at the throng of steerage passengers, she spotted someone she knew.

"Who is she?" I asked.

"A young Irish girl," he said. "She's around your age—maybe eighteen. Her name is Bridget."

"Or Bridie," I said without thinking. I hadn't told Charles about Sadie's discovery on the Boat Deck.

"Yes, for short. Anyway, she left my house without warning one day several months ago," Charles said. "It was only then I realized she'd stolen from me. She plans to bribe me with it, I'm sure."

"You're lucky you've found her," I said.

"Yes. You could say so," Charles replied. "I found out from the purser that she was scheduled to sail on the *Philadelphian*, but some of the steerage passengers were transferred to the *Titanic* at the last minute because of the coal strike. This is the only ship that had room for all the immigrants. They're coming in swarms, you know. You've seen them at home."

Irish men did most of the work in Charles' mills in Cleveland. The overseers called them terriers. The nickname was fitting, since they were worked like dogs in exchange for a pittance. The Irish had settled into a shanty town just down the hill from the docks called Whiskey Island. My mind traveled there briefly. I remembered all the times I had passed by in my carriage, watching the men return from work, dirty-faced and exhausted.

"Are you going to confront her when we get to New York?" I asked.

"I'm afraid we can't wait that long," Charles replied. "And that's where you come in."

I took a sip of my drink, hoping it would calm my nerves.

"I can't confront the girl myself," Charles continued. "It's far too risky for me to be skulking around in steerage. You're young. You can slip down there unnoticed."

I shook my head. "I can't be sneaking down to third class," I said, surprised by the forcefulness in my voice. "Why don't you send Rathbone? You pay him to do these things."

"Damn it, John, listen to me. I've willed you everything my father and I built, with no effort on your own part. Look around you," he said, motioning around the lavish first class smoking room. "What will you have if Lake Erie Steel is ruined? These documents are vitally important. For me…and for your future."

"What exactly do you want me to do?" I asked.

"I need you to find her," he said. "The steerage passengers gather in the third class lounge every night. It's the only place they can mingle, since the men's quarters are in the bow of the ship and the women are in the stern. I want you to find out how much she wants for the safe return of my letter. When you have a deal negotiated, I'll send Rathbone to make the exchange."

"Do you think it's safe?"

"Oh, don't be afraid of the girl," Charles replied. "I don't plan to send you without security."

Charles glanced around to make sure no one was watching him. Then he pulled aside his jacket, where I could see the gleam of his pistol.

"Do this for your mother," Charles said. "With everything she's been through, the last thing she needs is a scandal that could ruin all of us."

I nodded. "Yes, sir. I understand."

"I'm to meet with Anton in the lounge. We'll talk more tomorrow," Charles said.

Then he pointed a finger at me. "And remember, this is between you and me."

I said nothing as he left. The smoking room attendant came and went, offering another round, and I absentmindedly waved him away. My mind raced. When I was at Oberlin, I had no idea what Charles was up to on the other side of the Atlantic. What was he hiding?

"Rough night, eh?"

I turned around to find Max Seligman standing behind me, sporting his usual jovial grin.

"I must not be good at hiding it," I replied.

"How are you at blackjack?" he asked. "We've got a game going over in the corner. Besides, there's someone who wants to meet you."

It had to be a better option than sitting alone in my stateroom, brooding over Charles and his secrets.

"Everyone, this is John Conkling," Max announced as I took my place at the card table. "He's Charles Conkling's son—you know, the head honcho of Lake Erie Steel."

"And your mother is the one with the necklace," said the card dealer. I looked at him in astonishment. He was a flamboyant Frenchman who looked like he belonged at the Monte Carlo Casino instead of the *Titanic.*

"Word travels fast," I replied.

He smirked. "I learn a lot while dealing cards."

"He's also a student," Max said. "Speaking of which…"

A blonde man sitting next to him greeted me. "I'm Rudy," he said, with a German accent so thick I could barely understand him. "A fellow scholar."

He flashed me a tentative smile.

"John's at Oberlin College," Max said. "Say, Rudy, where do you study?"

The German's face went blank, as if he had never heard such a question.

"I beg your pardon?" he asked, although it seemed he'd heard Max as clearly as I had.

"Your university?" Max asked again.

"Ah, yes, *university*," the German responded. He grinned again, nervously. "I am at the University of Leipzig in Saxony. It is one of the oldest universities in the world."

"What do you study?" I asked.

"Uh…"

He stalled again, glancing around the smoking room. Max and I shot each other confused glances.

"Art," he finally said. "Art, and literature."

I shrugged it off, blaming the long pause on his middling grasp of English. At any rate, I had bigger worries tonight…like my shady mission to third class.

"Rudy was telling me he met the LaRoes tonight," Max said, and then gave a little whistle. "Faye's a real beauty, ain't she?"

"But she is like an iceberg," Rudy replied. "She sparkles on the surface, but beneath, she is solid ice." The men at the table laughed, even the card dealer.

"I have to be going now," Rudy said. He shook my hand. "It was very nice to meet you, John."

Then he gave me a piercing stare, just long enough to make me uneasy.

"Something's not right with him," I said to Max as soon as Rudy was out of sight.

"I was thinking the same thing!" he replied. "I was going to ask your opinion. He's an odd character, for sure. Crazy Kraut kid."

"He's the first university student I've met who doesn't seem to know what university he attends," I said, and Max laughed. "And what was the real reason he wanted to meet me?"

"Your guess is as good as mine," Max replied. He chuckled again, although it was obvious we both felt unsettled.

"I think I'm going to turn in, too," I said as I lost a round of blackjack.

"I'll see you at dinner tomorrow night," Max said. "And, if you don't mind, would you put in a good word for me with Faye?"

"I think she despises me."

"Well, come back for another game tomorrow," Max replied.

"We'll see," I said. "Tonight's been strange enough."

Three

The *Titanic* docked in Ireland the next morning. As evening approached, I was with Mother and Sadie on our private promenade, watching the emerald green coast fade into the horizon.

Mother sipped on the tea Celia had prepared for her, an expensive shawl wrapped around her shoulders. After all these weeks, she was still prone to chills.

"I'm feeling a little better every day, John," she said with a wan smile. "I just hope it lasts. Sometimes, just when I think the tremors are finally gone…"

"We'll have a fresh start in Cleveland," I assured her. "Springtime is coming. In a few months, we can go to the beach."

One of Charles' three homes was at Lakeside, a resort on Lake Erie. We'd spent a week there last summer while Charles was in Europe for business. It was the last time I could remember seeing Mother truly happy — although I wasn't sure if the beach or Charles' absence had more to do with it.

Just then Charles strode through the door, already dressed in his eveningwear. He looked around the promenade, visibly irritated.

"Victoria!" he barked. "Dinner is in thirty minutes. Let's get a move-on, shall we?"

"Yes, sir," Mother and Celia murmured in unison.

"And Celia, get Sadie dressed, for Christ's sake," Charles continued. "Wash her face."

"I don't want to go," Sadie whined. Her protests were ignored.

"And you," Charles said, motioning towards me. "Come with me."

He placed a hand on my shoulder, glancing behind him to make sure the others had gone inside before he spoke.

"I've found her," he said in a low voice.

"Bridget?"

"Who the hell do you think?" Charles snapped. "Yes, I found the girl. So let's have a look, why don't we?"

We took the staircase to A-Deck. From there, we could look down at the third class promenade, where the steerage passengers gathered. Some of them stood at the rails, watching the vast trail of churning ocean water as the propellers drove us toward New York. But mostly they congregated in relaxed circles, having a good old time—joking, laughing, puffing on cigarettes.

For a moment, I almost wished I could be among them.

Charles pointed. "There she is," he said. "With her back turned to us."

I noticed a girl, thin-boned and petite, standing with her hands braced against the railing. Her dress was simple, but an embroidered shawl covered most of her hair. Beside her was a man who touched her arm lightly as they spoke. They had the same hair color—dark, nearly black, with an auburn sheen.

"Who is that with her?" I asked.

Suddenly, as if they'd heard me from a distance, the pair turned toward us.

"Quick!" Charles said, ducking. "Don't let her see you!"

"Well, that did no good," I grumbled as we ducked back inside. "I barely got a look at her face." I tried to create a mental image of the girl along the railing. Under her dress, her shoulders were narrow, like a bird's.

I thought back to Sadie pointing at the seagull and saying, *Bridie.*

"Well, now what?" I asked.

"Like I said, you'll probably find her in the third class lounge tonight," Charles said. "Now, let's dress for dinner."

"Oh, one more thing," Charles said as we parted ways outside our staterooms. "You won't want to forget this." When no one was looking, he slipped me the pistol.

*   *   *

"Charles, are you sure my necklace is safe with the purser?" Mother asked on the way to dinner. She was frowning. "It would be dreadful if anything happened to it."

32

"Of course it is," Charles replied. "Frankly, it's more secure there than in our cabin."

It was strange that Charles insisted upon leaving Mother's diamond necklace with the purser. He used to encourage her to flaunt it. But now, he wanted it safely locked away.

He doesn't trust her anymore, I thought. These nagging feelings were getting tougher to ignore.

Dinner dragged on uneventfully. I half-listened to Max's European adventure stories and Anton's boasting about Gregory Galleries. I noticed Max trying to make eyes with Faye, who stared at her food, disinterested.

But mostly I watched the clock. It counted down the time until my mission in third class began. Even with Charles' gun secure inside my jacket, I was growing more nervous by the minute.

Charles nudged me under the table.

"John," he hissed. "Don't look so distracted."

"Sorry, sir," I grumbled, resisting the urge to elbow him back.

*   *   *

Charles had told me how to get into steerage. As soon as dinner ended, I made my way to the first-class elevator, where a lift attendant stood at the ready.

"Which way, good sir?" the young Englishman asked.

"I'm going to the third-class lounge."

I avoided eye contact with him, afraid he'd know I was off to some place I shouldn't be.

"Slumming, are we?" the attendant joked.

"Slumming" was what the rich passengers called it when they went down to steerage to gawk at the immigrants and partake in their drinking and dancing. It was a tacky pastime if you asked me. I nodded, trying to hide my disgust.

"Step this way," he said. "E-Deck it is."

The elevator glided downward. I had never been this far into the ship.

"Here we are," the lift attendant said as we came to a halt. "Through those doors is Scotland Road, which runs the length of the ship. Makes it easy for the crew to get from one end to the other. If you take it toward the stern, you'll reach the second class stairs, which will take you down to third class."

I followed Scotland Road until I came to a cast-iron gate, where the only person in sight stood. He was dressed in a White Star Line uniform.

"You can't go down there, sir," he said, observing my clothes. "I'm locking up for the night."

"I have important business to address," I replied, lifting my chin. I figured a hint of first class snobbery in my tone might get me past him.

He shrugged. "If you say so," he said.

The gate groaned as it swung open. I stepped down into a narrow corridor, lit by bright, bare bulbs. Compared to the elaborate beauty of first class, it had the feel of a warehouse. Some of the steerage passengers spoke in languages I'd never heard before—not even when I passed by the foreign language classrooms at Oberlin.

I didn't need to ask which way the lounge was after all. I spotted a rowdy gaggle of young passengers coming toward me, roughhousing and talking loudly. They passed around a flask.

"Ah, the sea and the whiskey are both smooth for a change," one of the boys said as he took a swig. "Have a drink! We're celebrating our new lives tonight, boys."

I followed them down the stairs to a dim room that reeked of smoke, beer, and merriment. My eyes began to sting. Before I reached the bottom of the stairwell, I could feel the floor vibrating beneath me in a steady beat. A band sat at the center of the lounge, where a man's voice bellowed even louder than the drum.

"I counted out me money and it made a pretty penny. I put it in me pocket and I took it home to Jenny."

If the girl I'd seen on the deck earlier that day was here, it was too dark and smoky to tell.

Someone bumped my arm as I watched the raucous scene around me.

"Oh! I'm sorry, my dear," said a redheaded girl, carrying a glass of beer in each hand. Then she gave me a second glance. "Hey, you don't look like you belong down here."

Caught, I thought, drawing a deep breath. I might as well tell her the truth.

"I'm looking for someone," I said. "She's an Irish girl, our age or so. Her name's Bridget."

"You mean that Bridget?" the girl replied, pointing straight ahead. "She's my bunkmate."

I spotted a girl dancing with a big man, who spun her around with drunken glee, nearly lifting her off her feet. They were both laughing.

"Yes, that's her," I said, my heart rate jumping.

"Bridget!" the redheaded girl shouted. "Come over here, will you?"

Bridget's eyes met mine, and her lips parted in shock. I took a few steps toward her, silently cursing Charles for sending me here. How was I supposed to introduce myself? *"I'm John Conkling and you've put my inheritance in jeopardy"*?

Before I could speak, a sharp blow landed against my stomach. A knee landed in my back, forcefully enough to throw me against the wall of the lounge. I heard myself gasp with pain.

Someone yanked me by the collar and dragged me to my feet. I felt another sharp sting as his fist hit me again.

"What did I tell you, Bridie?" a man's voice shouted. "I knew he was too big a coward to come here himself. He sent this little henchman instead!"

I opened my eyes. In front of me was the same man I'd seen on the deck that day, his dark sideburns and scowling expression unmistakable. Up close, his face looked just like Bridget's.

"Stop, Jim!" Bridget cried, grabbing his hand as it reached for me. She stared me down.

"Mr. Conkling...you're his son, aren't you?" she asked. "I had a feeling he'd send you."

I steadied myself on my feet, brushing the welt that was forming on my forehead. I stared at the Irish man in front of me, who clenched his fists with rage.

"He didn't say there'd be two of you," I said.

"I'm her brother," the man snapped. "And Conkling won't be causing her no more trouble. She was his maid and him trying to make her his left-handed wife…"

"Enough!" Bridget demanded.

"And if you're here for the letter, you tell him I'll chuck it into the ocean," Jim said. "…Unless he's willing to give me sister something to get her started in America."

I glanced around and realized Jim was flanked by two other boys. One merely glared at me. The other was grinding his fist against his palm, looking more than eager to use it.

They must have been the ones who hit me. I felt the welt on my forehead begin to throb. I steeled myself, trying to appear as calm as possible before I spoke.

"How much do you want for the letter?" I asked.

"Five thousand," Jim said. "That's enough to get her back on her feet."

I looked at Bridget. Her eyes searched my face for a moment, and then she stared at the floor.

"I'll need to meet with your sister privately to deliver the money," I said.

"Oh no you won't. You —"

"Jim, shut up!" Bridget said, exasperated.

"I'll take the offer to Charles," I said after a few long seconds of silence. "But I can't promise he'll take it."

Bridget finally looked up at me. I could see her eyes in the haze of the lounge. They were green, almost the same shade as Sadie's dress. "It's his only chance," she said, just firmly enough that I knew she meant it. "Meet me before we land."

Her brother jabbed his finger in my face.

"Five thousand dollars," he said again. "Next to what he has it's a bloody bargain. Then he'll get his damn letter, agreed?"

"Agreed."

"If not, I'll make sure you'll come to regret it, you hear?" Jim shouted after me as I walked away.

*   *   *

I took the elevator back to A-Deck, where Charles was waiting for me in the smoking room. I dreaded telling him about my utterly failed mission to steerage and about Jim's plan to hold the letter hostage.

I found him, drink in hand, sitting in the back corner with Anton.

Christ, why is he here? I wondered. Fabulously wealthy gallery owner or not, he gave me the creeps. And Charles had insisted this was between the two of us…not the two of us and his shady friend.

They stopped talking as soon as they noticed me walk in. "What happened to you?" Charles asked scornfully.

"Bridget's brother pounded me," I replied.
"I should have known."

"A warning would have been nice," I said.
"You never mentioned he was on board."

"That's because I didn't know the little
bastard *was* on board," Charles snapped.
"And I mean *bastard* in the literal sense; those
two have no father to speak of. I haven't seen
the brother since he was lurking around my
house making trouble."

Anton offered us cigarettes. I shook my
head. Charles lit his and leaned back in his
seat.

"I take it you didn't get the letter," he
said.

"They want five thousand dollars for it."

"Five thousand!" Charles slammed his fist
against the table. "So it's a ransom. They're
stupid to think I'd part with that kind of
money, especially for them."

"Her brother demanded it," I replied. "He
says she needs something to get her started in
America." I thought of asking Charles why
Bridget would quit working for him so
suddenly, but decided to leave it alone. It was
unlikely I'd get the truth out of him, anyway.

Some of the other smoking room patrons
glanced at us. Charles composed himself and
lowered his voice.

"Anton," he said. "Care to share a piece of
your mind? You've certainly dealt with your
share of thieves and tricksters over the years."

Anton thought for a moment, his brows lowering.

"Try to get the girl alone, without her brother," he suggested. "The steerage men are kept at the bow of the ship, the women and children at the stern. The ladies even have a matron to ensure the boys stay out of their bunks."

He and Charles laughed haughtily.

"Wait for her to return to her room, and then confront her." He nodded toward the slight bulge of the pistol under my jacket. "I suspect she'll concede quite quickly without her guardian. She hands over the letter, and the matter is settled."

"I don't know where her cabin is," I said.

"Incidentally, I do," Charles replied. "Rathbone got it from the purser. She's on F-Deck."

He pulled a folded piece of paper from his jacket and passed it to me. The purser had scrawled Bridget's cabin number on it.

"Go tomorrow night," Charles said.

"Alright," I said. "I'm going to bed. Goodnight."

*   *   *

Instead, I went to the Grand Staircase. I needed time to think before I could turn in for the night. After my encounter with Jim and his friends, adrenaline was still pumping through my veins.

At the landing of the Grand Staircase was a magnificent clock. I stopped to study it, admiring the intricate oak woodwork. Two women in Grecian robes were carved into the clock's face.

"Honor and glory," I heard a voice behind me say.

I turned around. It was Rudy, the German. He'd appeared out of nowhere.

"What?" I said, startled.

"Honor and Glory, crowning time," he repeated, pointing to the oak carving of the women draped around the clock.

"I know *that*," I snapped. "I've studied mythology. What are *you* doing here? Are you following me?"

"What?" he stammered. "Oh, no, no. Of course I'm not following you."

His response sounded rehearsed, as if he were feigning surprise at my hostile question.

"Actually, I don't even remember your name," Rudy said.

"John Merr—" Unconsciously, I started to introduce myself by my father's name.

Why did that nearly slip out? I wondered. Ever since Mother had married Charles, she'd encouraged me to abandon that name, to forget I ever answered to it.

"John Conkling," I corrected myself.

"Ah," Rudy said, nodding. "It's been nice to make a few new acquaintances on board. I'm alone on this trip. Also, we have something in common. We are both students."

Max and I both doubted that story last night. But in the interest of getting away from Rudy as fast as possible, I didn't challenge him. Besides, his studies — fictitious or not — were of no consequence to me. I had plenty of other things on my mind.

"But you do not seem in the mood to talk," he added. "Goodnight, John." He tilted his chin and gave me another unnerving smile.

Just like with Anton, I didn't know what it was about Rudy's presence that made me jumpy. I felt goosebumps forming on my arms.

Instead of returning to my room, I stood on the staircase for a few minutes, wanting to be sure that Rudy was gone. Then I slowly headed back toward the smoking room. I figured Charles and Anton had left for the night.

I spotted Max Seligman in the back corner, playing blackjack.

"Max!" I said, interrupting his game. "Do you know anything about that German?"

"Whoa, John, hold your horses," Max replied. "Sit down. What happened?"

"The German guy, Rudy," I said.

"I know who you're talking about," Max said. "How could I forget?"

"Well, I just ran into him in the Grand Staircase," I said. "…All by himself. It seemed like he was following me."

"I saw him flirting with Faye LaRoe earlier," Max said bitterly. "Maybe he thinks you're his ticket into her favors. Lord knows I haven't had any luck."

I laughed. "Hell will freeze over before that guy has a chance with Faye."

"He's an odd duck, I'll say," Max said. "But it's not just him. A lot of things about this ship give me the heebie-jeebies. Did you hear about our near-accident yesterday morning?"

"I saw it," I replied. "I was on the Boat Deck with Sadie."

"The same thing just happened to the *Titanic*'s sister ship, the *Olympic*," Max said, "except it actually hit. The *Olympic* sucked a helpless little cruiser right into her hull."

"You don't say."

"Yeah," Max replied. "So now the *Olympic* is laid up for repairs. Makes you wonder if White Star is testing its luck, making these ships so big. Too big."

"They insist the *Titanic* is unsinkable," I said.

"I know. But do you want to hear something really creepy?"

"What?"

44

"About fifteen years ago, some guy wrote a book called *Futility*," Max said. "It's about a ship designed to be 'unsinkable,' but she hits an iceberg and sinks in the North Atlantic with everyone aboard — men, women, children."

Even the other card players were listening now, eyebrows raised.

"And get this. The ship is called," he said, with a dramatic pause, "The *Titan*."

Once again, I felt goosebumps forming on my arms.

"It's a good thing I'm not superstitious," I replied. "That is creepy, though."

Max looked up at me with a more earnest expression. "Speaking of creepy, your father was in here earlier. What's he doing hanging around with Gregory?"

"Anton? They're friends, I guess," I said. "They met in London."

"Gregory's notorious among the businessmen aboard," Max replied. "He's crossed a lot of people. Nothing but trouble, I'm telling you. Conkling had better watch his back."

"That doesn't surprise me," I said. "I'll try to warn Charles."

Secretly, I was starting to sense I needed to watch my back, too.

Four

Mother didn't show up to lunch the next day.

"Where's Victoria?" Max asked Charles as we took our seats in the dining room.

"She was feeling ill this morning," Charles replied. "A touch of the mal de mer, I suspect." He sounded blasé.

I resisted rolling my eyes at Charles' pomposity. *Mal de mer*? Why couldn't he just say "seasickness"?

"However, gentlemen, we have a special guest joining us for lunch today," Charles said. "This is Thomas Andrews, the *Titanic*'s designer."

"Nice to meet you all," Andrews said, as he extended his hand to each of us. His Irish brogue was refined, far more graceful than the gruff accents of the steerage men I'd encountered down below.

"So, Mr. Andrews, the papers described this ship as 'unsinkable,'" Charles said. "How did you design a ship that can't sink?"

"It's quite simple, really," Andrews said. "The hull of the ship is divided into sixteen watertight compartments that reach all the way up to E-Deck."

Andrews moved his hands as he spoke, as if to help us visualize the bowels of the ship.

"In an emergency, the watertight doors will shut, either automatically when the water reaches a certain height, or electronically from the bridge," he continued. "*Titanic* can stay afloat with any two compartments or all four of the first compartments flooded. Even if our worst nightmare—a head-on collision with another liner—came to pass, we'd be able to stay afloat two days, three at the most."

"It certainly is a technological wonder," Charles said. "But it makes me question why they still thought it necessary to outfit us with lifeboats for everyone aboard. It's nonsensical to congest the deck space with those ugly wooden boats."

"There's enough for about half, actually," Andrews replied. "Some argued for no lifeboats at all, but the law requires them. If there was an emergency, the women and children would be put into the boats, while the men await the rescue ship."

Just then, I spotted Mr. Bowen, the steward, coming toward us.

"Yes, what is it?" Charles asked before he could even open his mouth.

"Your wife, sir," Mr. Bowen said. "She's quite ill and has requested your return to the stateroom."

Charles clucked with annoyance. "But we just sat down!" he replied. "I think she can wait until lunch is over."

"But…"

He turned back to our tablemates. "Sorry for the interruption, gentlemen," he said, in a tone that conveyed his disdain for Mother and her silly complaints.

I pushed away my plate and rose from my seat. "I'll go," I said, without hesitation.

"John…" Charles began, but I ignored him.

*   *   *

Mother was lying in bed by the time I reached B-Deck. Celia stood over her, holding a dampened cloth to her forehead. Sadie wandered into the room, clutching her doll.

"Johnny, why is Mommy sick?" she asked.

"Mommy's fine," I replied. "She's just tired."

"No she's not," Sadie insisted. "She fell again."

Mother moaned weakly.

"I've had enough of this," I muttered under my breath. It was clear that Charles was wrong to drag Mother on this voyage against the doctor's orders. He had such little regard for her that she was back at square one, confined to bed.

Just then, the door swung open abruptly.

"John, I need to talk to you," Charles said. "Privately."

"What is it?" I asked as I stepped into his stateroom. "To be frank, I'm more concerned with Mother right now."

"That's the nurse's job," Charles snapped. "We have to talk about tonight. I've thought it over, and I'll give Bridget half the money."

My mouth nearly fell open. After last night's tirade, the last thing I expected was for Charles to budge even an inch. I wondered what could have changed his mind. Whatever information was in that document, it must be damning.

"But I want to see the letter first to verify its authenticity," he continued. "If I'm satisfied, I'll send Rathbone with the cash."

"You know Jim and Bridget don't trust you," I replied. "I doubt they'll hand over the letter first."

"You're mistakenly assuming they're as bright as we," Charles replied haughtily.

I pictured the small, dark-haired girl I'd met last night, and felt an unexpected flash of anger that Charles kept belittling her. It was a strange sensation. *Why do I care what he says about her?* I wondered. *I don't even know her, and besides, she hates me already.*

"Fine," I said. "I'll try to get the letter tonight. Provided I don't get beat up again."

*   *   *

When I returned to Mother's stateroom, Celia ordered me out.

"John, keep Sadie busy for a while," she said. "Your mother needs to rest."

I took my sister's hand. "Would you like to get some tea and scones?" I asked. I pointed to her doll. "Dolly can come too."

Hesitantly, she nodded.

I led her to the Café Parisian on B-Deck, which was modeled after a French sidewalk café. It was filled with first class women sipping tea at sparkling white tables with red tablecloths. Sadie and I took a seat under a porthole, where the sun streamed in.

A café attendant came by to pour tea.

"Mommy's sick," Sadie said. "That means Daddy's angry again." Her nonchalant tone was chilling. At seven years old, she was becoming accustomed to this madness.

I set down my teacup and decided to see what else my sister knew.

"Sadie, how do you know Daddy's mad?" I asked.

She held a scone up to the doll's mouth, pretending to let it take a bite. "He yells a lot," she replied. "And he told Mr. Rathbone that Mommy was going away soon."

I wasn't sure if I heard her right. "He said *what*?"

"He said she was going away soon," Sadie repeated matter-of-factly.

My blood ran cold. *No, no,* I thought. Sadie had to be imagining things. Charles was arrogant, and a brute, but he couldn't possibly go that far…could he?

"What does that mean, Johnny?" Sadie asked. "Is it my fault for being naughty? I know I've been bad, but I don't want Mommy to leave me."

I decided it was best to calm her fears, at least for now. The last thing Mother needed was another tantrum.

"Of course it's not your fault," I said. "He probably just meant we were going home soon. All of us."

She shrugged.

"Okay," she said. "I don't like Daddy very much anymore."

"Me neither," I replied honestly.

Then she propped her doll in her lap and gazed up at me, her eyes dark and deadly serious. "Johnny, do you promise everything will be alright? I promise I won't be bad anymore."

I took her hand and forced myself to smile at her.

"Yes, Sadie. I promise."

*   *   *

After dinner, when the other first class passengers had retreated to the lounge or the smoking room, I again took the elevator to E-Deck.

It was late enough that the stewards would bar the third class men from the women's quarters. I hoped they'd already escorted the girls back to their cabins, said their good-byes and turned them in for the night.

"Slumming again?" the lift attendant asked. He took note of my bruises. "Didn't turn out so well last time, did it?"

"Just take me down, please," I replied.

I had the slip of paper with Bridget's cabin number: F-28. I followed Scotland Road to the third class stairwell, which took me into the lower decks of the ship.

The hallways were mostly empty, but I could hear the faint echo of music coming from one of the decks above. The steerage passengers must have gathered in the lounge again. I made my way to F-Deck, where I counted down the cabin numbers.

F-22. F-24. F-26. This next one has to be hers.

All of a sudden I heard a man's voice echoing in the stairwell behind me. I dodged into a nearby corridor and pressed myself against the wall, motionless. *Please, please don't let that be Jim*, I pleaded silently.

The voice was trailed by a girl's laughter.

"But I was winning!" she giggled. "You should've let me stay."

"Not until you learn to hold your liquor," the man responded, but his voice was pleasant. I heard a pair of keys enter the door lock as someone jiggled it open.

I peered around the corner. It was Bridget's bunkmate, her cheeks flushed and her red bun disheveled. With her was the same redheaded boy who had hit me. Jim's friend.

I pressed myself back against the wall.

"Goodnight, Mary," the redhead said. "Stay out of trouble, ya hear?" I held my breath as his heavy boots pounded back up the stairwell.

A few seconds later, I heard a door open again.

"I saw you back there," Mary's voice called. "You don't have to hide."

I stepped back into the hallway and smiled self-consciously, embarrassed that she'd caught me.

"I wasn't hiding," I explained hurriedly. "It's just that, you know, you had a man with you…"

"Patrick?" Mary interrupted. "He's my brother. And you needn't worry about him. He's harmless, so long as you keep him away from the other boys…and the Jameson."

She put her hands on her hips and studied me.

"So what's going on here?" she asked. "Last night wasn't a pretty sight. But here you are, back for more. You must have a good reason for it."

"It's a long story," I replied. "Do you know where she is? I need to talk to her alone."

"She's in the smoking room with the boys," Mary said. "They've got a horse race going on. I was winning until Patrick turned me in for the night. Do you know the game, horse racing?"

I shook my head.

"Figures," Mary said, noting my neat grooming and expensive clothes. "Well, she'll be back here soon, but I can't promise Jim won't be with her."

"Thanks, Mary," I said. And with that, she went back into the small cabin she shared with Bridget.

There was no chance I was going to the smoking room, which was surely filled with drunk Irishmen willing to fight me. Instead, I waited. Groups of women came and went, some escorted by men. Others were hand-in-hand with children. I gathered that most of the steerage passengers were Irish or Scandinavian—Swedish, maybe. They called back and forth to one another in their singsong language. None noticed me.

Finally, I heard a girl humming to herself softly as she approached. I hesitated, listening for a man's boots pounding on the steps behind her. There were none.

Bridget halted in her tracks when she saw me. "What are you doing here?" she demanded. "How'd you find my cabin?"

"I need the letter," I said, ignoring her questions.

"I don't have it," she replied, inching towards her door. "Please, just leave me alone."

"Then why did you demand five thousand from Charles?"

"Don't ask me," she said. "It was Jim's idea to steal the letter, after I told him what it said. He has it."

"In his cabin?" I asked, trying to stall her until she relaxed.

Suddenly a voice called out from the top of the stairwell. "Bridget? Is that you?"

"Oh, no," Bridget breathed. "My brother's coming!"

"Are you down there, Bridget?" Jim called again.

She grabbed my sleeve. "This way!" she said. She guided me through the maze of steerage hallways with ease.

"Up these stairs," Bridget said. "We'll go outside."

We climbed the stairwell to the third class promenade, where a few steerage passengers gathered in the cold, smoking and taking in the ocean air. I scanned their faces to see if the Irish boys had followed us, but they were nowhere in sight.

"That was close," Bridget said, heaving a deep sigh of relief.

"I take it your brother doesn't like me much," I said. "He left me with a nasty bump last night."

Bridget laughed. "It's your father he doesn't like much," she admitted.

She looked up at me. "I used to dust your family portraits in the house," she said. "When I saw you in the lounge, I knew you must be his son."

I didn't bother to correct her. If he talked about me at all, Charles must not have mentioned that I was really his stepson.

"Charles wants to make a deal for the letter," I said. "But first, I have to know what it says. Why did Jim want to steal it?"

"I can't tell you," she replied stubbornly.

"Bridget, please," I said. "Charles won't tell me himself. I can't imagine what trouble he's in, but I had nothing to do with it. I'm his heir. Whatever that letter says, it will fall on my shoulders someday."

She paused for a moment.

"I didn't mean to see it," she finally said. "But sometimes Mrs. Conkling asked me to open the mail. It was a letter from the engineers up at the mill. Mr. Conkling's company has been making bad steel. High in sulfur, it said. And they put it in the *Titanic*!"

"The shipyards don't know the steel is no good," she said. "It'd be a scandal if anyone knew."

The huckster! That's what Charles was hiding. He'd been selling cheap steel to the shipyards for a hefty profit, knowing it was junk. And now he was trying to cover his tracks.

"It could put Lake Erie Steel out of business, that's for certain," I said. "How did you end up working for Charles, anyway?"

"Jim was looking for factory work in London last fall," Bridget said. "So I went there to join him after my mama died. A girl I met, another Irish girl, worked for a family friend of the Conkling's. They hired me to take care of Sadie and do the domestic work. The Conklings, I thought they were so kind…"

Bridget's voice trailed off, and she looked down at her boots for a moment.

"…Anyway, like I said, it was Jim's idea to bribe Mr. Conkling," she continued. "I told him what the letter said, since he can't read. Jim told me to write a note saying we'd give it to the papers. I put it on his desk, and then I took off for good."

"We need the money, of course," Bridget said. "But above all, I think Jim wants to punish Mr. Conkling."

"For what?" I asked.

She shuddered and shook her head, as if to erase the thought. Then she looked at me defiantly.

"Jim says I'm not to trust you," she said.

"Fair enough." I sensed that I couldn't get anywhere by arguing with her.

We stayed silent for a minute, staring out into the water.

"It's hard to believe you're a Conkling," Bridget finally said.

"Why is that?"

"I just don't see much of Mr. Conkling in you," Bridget said, studying my face.

I opened my mouth to explain that Charles wasn't my father—that my real father passed away years ago. I was cut off by an angry voice.

"You!"

I spun around to find Jim stalking toward me. The two boys who'd been there last night followed close behind.

I put my hands up to show I wasn't looking for a fight. "Please," I said. "We're just working out a deal."

"Shut up, you ninny."

And with that Jim flung me into the railing. As my head crashed against the iron, he hit me again.

"Get him, boys!"

Bridget screamed. The redhead tried to drag me back onto my feet, no doubt so he could knock me down again.

"Where's the money?" Jim shouted.

"I don't have it yet!"

"Then you tell that dirty old man to cough it up or I'll—"

Suddenly another voice interrupted, calm but forceful.

"Jim! Stop that right now! *Right. Now!*"

It was a man dressed in a long black robe with a white collar. A cross hung around his neck.

"Sorry, Father Byles," Jim grumbled. He let go of my clothes and let me sink back to the ground.

"What are the three of you doing beating up on this one young lad? What did I tell you about the fighting?" the priest demanded, but his voice wasn't angry. He reached out and helped me up.

"Jim, you reek of whiskey," he said. "Hitting the bottle for the third night running, aye?"

The boys stared at their feet in shame.

"Go back to your cabins," Father Byles said. "Take Barry and Patrick with you. No more liquor tonight."

"Yes, Father." The boys quietly retreated toward the staircase. After he watched them go, the priest retreated, too.

"Good night, Bridget," he said, and shot me a look. "Be more careful from now on."

Bridget turned back to me and shook her head.

"He's the only man on the ship the boys will listen to," she explained. "He warned Jim about the fighting. Our first night on board, the master-at-arms had him in handcuffs. He got drunk and took a swing at a boy who got too close to me in the lounge."

She laughed, but I changed the subject. I was subconsciously aware of the time. Charles would be waiting for me by now, and I couldn't afford to make him suspicious.

"Listen, Bridget, I have to get that letter," I said. "I didn't sell the bad steel. But if Lake Erie goes under, I'm ruined, too. Charles wants to see it before he gives you the money. Can you get it from Jim?"

The wind was bitterly cold. Bridget lifted the shawl from around her shoulders and draped it around her hair, shivering.

"I know my brother won't give it up without seeing the money first," she said. "If I could, I would."

I could tell by the look on her face that she meant it. The deck lights shone on her face, illuminating the glints of red in her hair and the green in her eyes.

"What if I bring the money?" I asked. "Can we meet again tomorrow?"

She nodded. "I'll tell Jim."

"I can send you a message through the stewards," I said. "I'll give you a time and a place to meet. You can bring your brother if you'd like, but tell him I'll have the money."

60

"We can't go into first class," she reminded me. "It's the law aboard ships. The English think we're all crawling with disease." She wrinkled her nose in disgust.

"I can come back down to steerage," I offered. "First class passengers do it all the time."

Bridget looked me over.

"Yeah, and they stand out like a sore thumb," she retorted. "If you don't want to call attention to yourself, you'll not want to come looking like this again." She pointed to my neatly pressed clothes, which I'd worn to dinner in first class. "Come with me."

She led me to the third class stairs, back down to F-Deck. She rapped lightly on her cabin door.

"Mary, are you asleep?" she called. There was no answer.

Bridget swung the door open and flipped on the light.

"She ran off again!" she laughed. "Oh, Mary. She met a boy in the smoking room our first night on board, and she's been sneaking down to the boys' cabins to see him. I hope they don't catch her."

She turned back to me. "Then again, I'm not allowed to have you in my bunk, either," she said with a raised eyebrow.

I had never been inside a girl's bedroom before, aboard a ship or elsewhere. I could feel myself blushing.

"Well, shut the door before someone sees you!" she said.

I stepped inside. It was a cramped cabin. The only amenities were a wash basin and two sets of bunks. It was a far cry from my elegant stateroom in first class.

"Mary and I share this bunk," she said, motioning to the right side of the room. "Two other girls sleep over there, but they don't speak English."

She reached under the lower bunk and pulled out a soft bundle.

"I packed some of Jim's clothes," Bridget said. "Before you come down here again, put this jacket on. Pull the hat over your hair."

I opened the package. Inside were worn clothes and a threadbare cap, the same kind Jim had been wearing tonight. They smelled of smoke.

"You're right," I said. "No one will recognize me in this." *Besides Jim,* I thought, *who will probably flip his lid at the sight of me wearing his clothes.*

There were women's voices outside the door.

"It's the other bunkmates," Bridget said. "Go! Send me a message through the stewards. I'll send one back as quick as I can." She opened the door and gave me a light shove. I nearly collided with two Scandinavian women, who looked baffled by my presence.

"Excuse me, ladies," I said in a language they couldn't understand. I brushed past them and hurried back up the stairs.

The gate was locked, and the hallway was empty. I'd have to get back through the deck. I found my way outside and up the stairs to the promenade, where I climbed over the gate that read, in bold letters: "No third class passengers allowed beyond this point."

As soon as I steadied myself on the deck, I felt someone grab me by the collar.

"I saw that."

It was Charles. He glowered at me, tightening his grip until I grabbed his wrist and thrust it away.

"Saw what?" I asked angrily.

"I sent you down there to get my property, not to stand around on the steerage deck making eyes at her," he snarled.

"It sounds like you made more than eyes at her," I replied. I thought of what Jim had called him, and it made my skin crawl: *that dirty old man.*

For a moment I braced myself for a fistfight. I wouldn't be sucker-punched this time, like I was by Jim.

"Where's the letter?"

"She doesn't have it," I replied. "She says it's in her brother's cabin. There's no getting around him, Charles. He wants the money first."

"We'll see about that," he said. His tone became accusatory. "I don't think you understand the seriousness of this situation, John."

"Oh, I do," I said. "You've been selling bad steel. And they put it in the *Titanic*."

Charles was simmering with rage. I instinctively clenched my fists again, holding them at my sides.

"The steel I've been selling?" Charles replied. "As far as anyone's concerned, in a few years' time, it's the steel *you've* been selling. You're my successor. What do you have without me? Who pays your tuition, John?"

I bit my lip for a second, not sure how to proceed. On one hand, I was tired of being pushed around by him. On the other, I was afraid he would take his anger out on Mother.

"I offered to make the exchange tomorrow," I said. "Five thousand isn't much in order to save Lake Erie Steel from ruin."

Charles narrowed his eyes, thinking.

"Let me decide that," he replied carefully. "I'll see what Anton and I can come up with."

"Alright."

"And one more thing, John," he said. "Don't get any stupid ideas. No future president of Lake Erie Steel is going to be down in steerage getting starry-eyed over that trash."

"Goodnight, Charles," I said, turning my back to him.

*   *   *

The air on the Boat Deck was freezing, but the wind didn't blow. I wondered how fast the *Titanic* was going. Twenty knots, maybe. At this rate, we would be in New York by Tuesday.

And then I'd be out of time.

I wondered if my life would ever return to normal after this voyage. I thought of my friends back at Oberlin, who might be taking a break from studying with a bottle of gin tonight. I began to long for the times when my biggest worry was an upcoming exam. What would happen if Lake Erie Steel met a scandalous demise?

My thoughts were interrupted by the sound of laughter. I looked over my shoulder to see who else was crazy enough to be out in the cold. It was a man and a woman from first class—I could see the length of the woman's expensive-looking red dress underneath a black fur coat.

"I can't see the stars in Cleveland," a familiar voice said. "The lights from the city burn too brightly."

"Faye?" I exclaimed, shocked that she was out at this hour...with a man. As her

65

companion stepped into the light, I could see his face clearly.

It was Rudy.

"John!" Faye cried, gathering her composure as soon as she saw me. "What are you doing out here?"

"I'm avoiding my stepfather," I replied. "But I was wondering the same thing about you."

Faye's alabaster skin was now the color of her dress. I'd stumbled upon a furtive outing. It was obvious that Mrs. LaRoe didn't know Faye was missing from her stateroom. She'd have a conniption if she knew her daughter was with that creepy German.

"Have you met Rudy Gottlieb?" Faye asked.

"Yes, I've met John," Rudy answered for me. "We played blackjack together in the smoking room." He didn't mention our encounter in the Grand Staircase.

"I didn't know you two were...friends," I said. Maybe Max had been right, and Rudy's only motivation for meeting me was to get closer to her.

Faye looked at me shamefacedly. "You're not going to tell anyone, are you?" she asked.

"Your secret's safe with me," I replied. "No one knows I'm out here, either."

"By the way, John, I seem to have startled you in the Grand Staircase last night," Rudy said with a conciliatory smile. "My apologies." He sounded sincere for once.

"No apologies needed," I said. "But if you don't mind, I'm going to go back inside. Goodnight, Faye."

"Wait," Rudy replied. He stepped away from Faye. "Can we talk tomorrow?"

"Sure," I said. What did it matter if I agreed or not? He seemed to show up wherever I went. "What is it about?"

Rudy glanced around to make sure no one else was listening. Then, he leaned in and murmured, "Your stepfather."

Five

The next morning, I went to find the steward, Mr. Bowen.

"I need to deliver a message to someone," I said.

"Yes, of course," he replied, disinterested despite my urgent tone. "Do you have their cabin number? If not, I can look it up for you."

"F-28," I said. "It's third class."

Mr. Bowen cocked an eyebrow.

"Very well, then," he said, pretending not to be curious. "Write it on here."

I took the stationery adorned with White Star Line's logo. *Meet me at 10 outside your cabin*, I scribbled, and signed my name. I folded it before Mr. Bowen could see what I had written.

I hoped it wouldn't end up in the wrong hands.

As soon as Mr. Bowen was out of sight, I went to Charles' and Mother's stateroom. I found myself unconsciously crossing my fingers: *Please let her be alright*. We were halfway to Cleveland, and if Mother fell seriously ill now…

Inside the stateroom, Mother was ashen but sitting up in bed, sipping a cup of tea. In the center of the room, Celia had Sadie perched on a foot stool as she tugged at her hair, winding it into tight coils.

"It will only take a few more minutes, dear," Mother said from her bed. Sadie shrieked.

"Good God, Mother, would you stop with the curls?!" I yelled. "Can't you see she hates it?"

Sadie stopped crying. Mother and Celia stared up at me, stunned by my outburst. This wasn't like me, and they knew it.

The stress of becoming Charles' henchman was eating at me.

"Celia, take Sadie to her room," Mother ordered. The nurse quietly picked her up and carried her away. Half of her long brown hair was still pinned against her scalp, twisted so tightly that the sight of it made me wince.

"Sit down, Johnny," Mother said. I sank to the foot stool where Sadie had been sitting.

"I'm sorry, Mother," I said. "It's just that—"

"Quiet," she hissed. "Do you understand the pressure your stepfather heaps upon me? To measure up to the other passengers, when they know I've been ill? To have our child come to supper looking like a little doll?..."

Her voice wavered as her eyes flooded with tears.

"No one faults you for being sick, Mother." I could tell from the look in her eyes that she knew I was lying.

"You don't have to be everything Charles expects you to be, you know," I said. "Father never did this to you."

"Don't bring up your father, please," Mother said. "I don't want to hear about him today."

"You never want to hear about him," I said. "We stopped talking about him the day you married Charles. I can't even mention his name anymore." I thought of how I had almost slipped and called myself by Father's name the night I saw Rudy in the Grand Staircase.

We both stayed quiet for a moment.

"I'll come back to check on you later," I said. "I'm going to explore the ship for a bit."

"Wonderful," Mother replied. "And if you see Charles, can you tell him to come to me? I haven't seen him all morning."

"Of course," I said. But I suspected Charles had other plans for the day.

*   *   *

By late afternoon, I was starting to worry. I sat in a chair at the foot of the Grand Staircase, trying to collect my thoughts. Why wasn't Bridget responding to my message? She told me last night that she would write back, just before she shoved me out the door of her cabin. Had the stewards forgotten to give it to her? Or worse—had it fallen into Jim's hands?

I spotted Charles and Mr. Rathbone coming towards me. Charles' face looked tense, and their pace was oddly swift.

"Hello, John." Charles acknowledged me with nod, then quickly looked away. I opened my mouth to say that Mother wanted him, but before I could speak, they were already disappearing down the staircase.

Charles was bringing Rathbone into his plot. He no longer trusted me after he'd watched me with Bridget on the deck. I could still hear Charles' snarling.

I sent you down there to get my property, not to stand around on the third class deck making eyes at her.

They were going to Rathbone's cabin. I was certain of it.

I began to follow them.

I wondered, for a brief moment, what on Earth I was doing. I couldn't afford to anger Charles—not now, with Mother in such fragile condition. But I found myself trailing Charles and Rathbone anyway, walking quietly behind them to D-Deck. They were too absorbed in conversation to notice.

I ducked into another hallway when they entered Mr. Rathbone's stateroom. The door slammed, and keys rattled as it was locked from the inside.

Most of the time, Charles met with Rathbone or Anton in the smoking room, where he could sip on expensive liquor as he schemed. Now, he wanted absolute privacy.

I tiptoed up to the door, where I could hear their voices more clearly.

"You haven't retrieved the letter yet?" Mr. Rathbone asked.

"No, no," Charles said. There was a long pause and some rustling.

"Rathbone, I think I might have a traitor on my hands."

I was right. Charles was cutting me out of his plot.

"Don't look so startled," Charles said with a laugh. "I don't mean you."

"You mean John?"

I could hear Charles lighting up a cigarette. "John has resented me since the day I married Victoria," he said matter-of-factly. "I thought he'd come around, act like a son, show some interest in my business. Sarah is the only child Victoria's bore me in eight years, you know." Charles was the only person who called Sadie by her formal name, Sarah, instead of her nickname.

"However, I might have John in my clutches just long enough for him retrieve the letter," Charles said. "He's enjoying these little visits to the Irish tart. Perhaps a bit too much."

"It's a pity your plan to put Victoria away was a failure," Rathbone said.

"Don't remind me," Charles replied. "Victoria's crazy, but it seems she's not crazy enough for the asylum."

"I meant your second plan."

Charles laughed again. "At least the poison was enough to cause seizures," he said. "I believe it confirmed everyone's suspicions that she's unwell, mentally."

Charles was the one making her sick!

Everything about Mother's condition made sense now. Charles was poisoning her, and then making her out to be a hysteric when she fell ill. I resisted the urge to beat down the door, to confront him in a murderous rage. I fought with all my power to stay quiet.

"It's a shame she has such a hefty chunk of your steel profits about her neck," Rathbone said.

"You mean the necklace?" Charles replied. "Not anymore. She thinks it's with the purser."

"What did you do with it?"

"I gave it to Anton," Charles said. "When we get to New York, I will report it stolen. Of course, they'll never find the phantom thief, because Anton will sell the necklace for me. I agreed to give him a twenty percent commission. If the truth about the steel ever surfaces and Lake Erie Steel is ruined, I have insurance. From Anton's black market dealings, mind you."

"What about Victoria?"

"Oh, if she keeps up her dramatic performances, I'll have her put away for good," Charles replied blithely. "She'd make a fascinating case study for that Dr. Freud character. As you know, the law favors the husband in such matters. I'll take Sarah and find a new wife, perhaps one who will give me a son."

"I'm surprised you trust Anton to follow through with this plan," Rathbone said. "Is he aware that it's an act of fraud?"

"Anton's a greedy bastard," Charles replied. "He'll take that kind of risk for twenty percent. Especially now, with his, ahem, *special interests.*"

"And what about John?" Rathbone asked.

"John's not my son," Charles snapped. "When we get home and the divorce is underway, I plan to cut him out of my will. I owe the boy nothing. John is an intellectual, and intellectuals have no mind for business."

"If you're concerned about business, sir, you *need* to get that letter from your maid." Even Rathbone sounded uneasy with his brazenness.

There was another pause as they both dragged on their cigarettes. "You know, Charles, you ought to throw that ungrateful girl overboard."

"Thank you for mentioning that," Charles said. "She will no longer pose a threat to me, I assure you."

"Are you giving them the money?"

"Heavens, no. You know me better than that. But I will be getting that letter. I don't care if I have to kill for it."

"I like the way your mind works, Mr. Conkling."

I heard them both laugh wickedly.

*   *   *

I could feel my pulse pounding in my temples as I climbed the first class stairs. Who did I go to first? Mother? Bridget? Charles had it in for all of us.

I thought of how Mother had been bedridden yesterday. Was he trying to poison her now? Or was he waiting to divorce her when they got to Cleveland, as he'd told Rathbone?

If Charles had his way, Mother and I would never see Sadie again.

I had to get the necklace back and hide it. It was our only insurance against Charles.

I went to the staterooms on B-Deck. Charles' and Mother's door was unlocked, and I saw Mother in bed, her dark curls fanned out on the pillow. I raced to her in a panic.

"Mother?" I cried, grabbing her wrist.

There was a steady pulse. For now, she was fast asleep, dreaming peacefully.

Sadie and Celia's adjoining room was empty.

I caught a glimpse of the bureau where Charles and Mother kept their belongings. I opened the drawer, rifling through layers of clothing. If there was a vial of poison hidden there, I was determined to find it.

"What are you doing in here? Get out of my drawers!"

The sound of Charles' voice made me jump.

"I—I was just looking for a tie, sir," I stammered, knowing it was an obvious lie. "Dinner starts in an hour."

"A tie," he repeated sneeringly. "Is that so, John?"

Charles shoved me aside. He reached into the bureau and pulled out a red necktie.

"There you are," he said, and he threw it at me.

"Thank you, sir," I said. I was red-faced and visibly nervous. My hands shook as I snatched the tie from the floor.

"See you at dinner," Charles replied coldly. "By the way, I'm still waiting for my letter."

Faye sidled up to me outside of the dining room while our parents were distracted.

"Quick, John," she said, uncurling her fist to reveal a small slip of paper. "It's from Rudy."

I read it over: *Meet me at the squash court at 11 tonight.*

"The squash court?" I asked, scratching my head. "Is it even open that late at night?"

"He convinced the squash coach to reserve it for him," Faye replied. "He said no one will find you there, just in case."

She motioned subtly toward Charles.

"Good thinking," I said. "Faye, did Rudy tell you anything I should know? How does he know Charles' business?"

She shook her head. "He wouldn't tell me," she said. "Only that he must meet with you before we land. He said time is of the essence."

Her usual steely demeanor was gone. She looked worried. "Your family isn't in trouble, is it?" she asked.

"I hope not," I said, and slid the note into my pocket for safe keeping.

*   *   *

After dinner, I pulled out the bundle of clothing Bridget gave me last night, wrinkling my nose at the lingering cigarette odor. I noticed they were a bit smaller than my own clothes. For someone so slender, Jim threw a hard punch.

I decided not to take the elevator this time. The lift attendants might start to suspect me, questioning why I was going down to third class every evening. I would go to the Boat Deck and take the second class stairs, which led directly to Scotland Road.

Passengers milled about the deck, taking in the sunset. It was Saturday night, April thirteenth. I could hear the *Titanic*'s band playing in the lounge, a lively tune that would keep the first class passengers amused as they sipped their after-dinner drinks. They were too refined to dance the way they did in steerage, but it was a welcome diversion from the relentless pressure to keep up appearances.

The aft stairway was filled with second class passengers coming back from dinner. I slipped past them, confident that none would recognize me. I followed the winding staircase all the way down to E-Deck, where I could find my way into steerage.

At F-Deck, I took a deep breath and knocked on her cabin door.

"Bridget?" I called.

Nothing.

All of a sudden I heard someone rustling about in the room. I must have awoken her, because the footsteps were lethargic.

"It's John," I said through the door. "If you're in there, please come out."

The door swung open. It wasn't Bridget. Instead, one of the Scandinavian girls stood in the doorway. Our eyes met, although neither of us knew what to say.

"I'm sorry," I stuttered. "I was looking for Bridget."

She couldn't understand me.

"Bridget," I repeated.

With her free hand, she pointed towards the ceiling.

"Lounge," she said in broken English, thrusting her index finger into the air, towards the deck above.

"She went to the lounge?"

The girl nodded.

"Thank you, miss," I said, as she closed the door on me.

The third class lounge was quiet tonight. There were no pounding drums, no stomping feet—just a single man playing the piano at the center of the room. He sang a slow, sad Irish song.

"Oh Danny boy, the pipes, the pipes are calling…"

I caught a flash of Mary's red hair across the room. She was sitting between her brother and another young man, a pint of beer in front of each of them. As always, Mary was laughing.

"I had a feeling you'd be back!" she called when she saw me. "Have a beer, will you?"

I sat down at the table, feeling a little more at ease in steerage with each passing night. At least Mary was fond of me, in her bemused way.

"This is Brendan," she said, pointing to the boy on her right. "I met him when we got on board at Queenstown. He's going to be a policeman in America." She gave him a little kiss.

He must be the one she kept sneaking into the bow to see. He was a handsome enough fellow, and even somewhat polite. He shook my hand and said hello.

"And you've already met my brother Patrick. Well, his fist, anyhow," Mary snickered. "You can blame the Jameson."

"I'm looking for Bridget," I said. "Your bunkmate said I could find her here."

"Bridget hasn't been here at all tonight," Mary replied.

"Do you know where she is now?"

Mary shrugged. "She's with Jim somewhere," she said. "But the last I saw of them was at dinner. She seemed really worried about something."

I feigned cluelessness.

"I know she read your message today," Mary said. "'Tis a bit strange for girls like us to be getting letters from the likes of you. She was all starry-eyed over it."

"What?" I said, not sure how to take that comment. "So she *did* read it."

"Yeah, of course," Mary replied. She tilted her head, giving me a suspicious look.

"Are you ever going to tell me the real reason you're down here every night?" she asked. "I'm near dying of curiosity now."

"Unfinished business Bridget left behind in London," I said.

"Yeah, unfinished business with the lecher," Mary snickered. "Well, I don't know what to tell you. You could check the smoking room. She might be in the bow with Jim, but the stewards will kick her out sooner or later."

"Thanks, Mary," I said. I would have to steel myself and go to the smoking room.

*   *   *

The third class smoking room was filled with steerage men playing cards and horse racing. They bantered with each other loudly, taking big gulps of beer. I could barely see through the cigarette smoke.

"Hey, who are you looking for?" one of the men shouted at me in a British accent.

"Uh, Jim," I stammered. "And his sister."

"Jim," the man repeated, turning to the other card players. "That's the Irish bloke, ain't it? The one we horse raced with?"

"Aye, that's him."

"He's not here," the British man said. "Hasn't been here since last night. Hell, he's probably got a wicked hangover."

There was one more place to look. I went out onto the third class deck, which was nearly empty. The sky was black. The only sound I could hear was the *Titanic*'s propellers slicing through the Atlantic, leaving a ghostly white trail in her wake.

This mission was hopeless. Bridget was nowhere to be found, and I suspected she was purposely avoiding me. I'd have to go back to Charles and tell him once again that I didn't have the letter. How much more could I anger him during this voyage without crossing the line? How far could I go before Mother, Bridget, and Sadie were in danger?

For now, I shoved the thought out of my mind. I had to go meet with Rudy and find out what other dark secrets Charles was keeping.

*   *   *

The squash court was on the lowest deck of the ship, which were quiet at this hour. The first class passengers who were still awake were in the smoking room or the lounge.

Faye was right. It was highly unlikely that anyone would see Rudy and me, let alone question what we were doing there.

Still, I had butterflies in my stomach as I turned the knob on the squash court's heavy metal door. I knew that whatever Rudy had to tell me about Charles, it wasn't good.

"Thank you for coming," Rudy said as I stepped inside. His relaxed smile put me at ease. To my surprise, he handed me a racquet.

"I didn't know we were actually playing squash," I laughed.

"Of course. It makes us look sincere," he replied. "I was lucky that the squash instructor, Mr. Wright, let me reserve the court at this hour. Have you met Mr. Wright?"

I realized now that Rudy spoke nearly perfect English. He had been faking confusion in the smoking room when he seemed to forget which subjects he studied at Leipzig.

"No, I haven't met him," I said. "I haven't had much time for fun on this voyage."

"You indicated that last night," Rudy replied.

"So," I said, serving the ball, "are you going to tell me why we're here?"

"Yes. But first, let me explain who I am," Rudy said. "I presume you thought I was lying about being a student."

"I did," I answered honestly.

"Well, I did attend the University of Leipzig," he said. "But that was years ago.

These days, I work for the German government."

So? I thought, a little annoyed by his dramatics.

"Why did you have to keep that secret?" I asked. "There are plenty of government officials in first class. President Taft's military advisor, Archibald Butt, is on board."

Rudy's eyes darted around the squash court, even though we had a heavy steel door guarding us from eavesdroppers. "Because," he said slowly, "I'm not a government official, John. I'm a spy."

My eyes widened in disbelief. "You've been spying on Charles?" I asked. No wonder it seemed like he was following me. "Why?"

"That wasn't my intention," Rudy said. "My main interest is in Mr. Gregory, the gallery owner. As I'm sure you know, he's a smuggler."

"I've heard rumors that he smuggles art and jewelry," I said.

"Yes, that is true. But do you know what he does with the money?"

"Spends it on women and parties?" I guessed, really having no idea.

Rudy laughed wryly.

"Well, yes," he said. "He is also a major financier of a group in the Balkans...a group that calls itself the Black Hand."

"The revolutionary group?" I gasped. "I've heard about it at Oberlin! I never would have guessed Anton was linked to it, though. He told us he paid no attention to Serbian affairs."

Rudy clucked in disbelief.

"I've been watching Mr. Gregory very closely," he said. "I've especially watched his interactions with Mr. Conkling. I was able to eavesdrop on their conversation in the smoking room while I played cards."

"What did you learn?"

"When Anton sells the necklace, the money will be funneled to his Serbian friends," Rudy said. "They'll be one step closer to setting off a continent-wide war in Europe."

"Anton's not getting off the ship with that necklace," I replied. "I'm going to get it back somehow."

Rudy stared at me, awaiting an explanation. I couldn't offer one — at least not yet.

"When I have it, I'll let you know," I said.

"I'll be waiting," he replied cautiously. "Be very careful about crossing Mr. Gregory. If you need my help, come to me. My cabin is A-14."

He shook my hand, indicating that our meeting was over.

"I'm glad to have earned your friendship, John," he said. "I work for Germany, but if and when the war breaks out, I plan to take the Americans' side. I've always been fond of your people."

I smiled tentatively at him, apprehensive about what was in store for the remainder of the voyage. But no matter what, I was going to get the necklace.

"I have associates on board," Rudy said, "other men working for Berlin. I can't say much more, but I might be sequestered with my associates tomorrow. If you get the necklace, find me."

"I'll see you tomorrow," I said.

It was a promise.

Six

In the morning the sun shone brightly over the Atlantic. It was Sunday, April fourteenth, 1912. Captain Smith led a church service in the first class dining room. I was standing shoulder-to-shoulder with Charles, but we dared not talk to each other.

It was useless to speak, anyhow, when we could read each other's minds.

The Captain led us in the Navy Hymn, the lament of sailors in distress.

"Oh hear us when we cry to thee, for those in peril on the sea."

At least peril on the sea wasn't on my list of worries. My mind drifted back to Thomas Andrews explaining his unsinkable ship: *Even if our worst nightmare came to pass, we'd be able to stay afloat two days, three at the most.*

Just then, one of the wireless operators rushed up to Captain Smith holding a telegram.

"We got another one, sir," he said. "This one from the *Californian*."

Captain Smith gave it a cursory glance and shrugged before handing it back to the wireless operator.

"Thank you, Mr. Bride. Make sure to warn the bridge," he said. He turned back to me and Mother.

"Iceberg warnings," he explained. "They're quite common on this route during the spring."

"Will it be slowing us down?" Mother asked, frowning. "The trip has been lovely, but I'm eager to get home."

"Certainly not," Smith replied confidently. "We're making excellent time. In fact, Mr. Ismay, the president of the White Star Line, just requested that we increase our speed."

I saw Bruce Ismay every night in the dining room. He was a Brit with an ego proportionate to the size of the *Titanic*. It was like him to order us full speed ahead through the ice fields, probably hoping to set a record of some sort.

But I wasn't concerned about ice now. I knew time—and Charles—was working against me. I had to get the necklace before it was too late.

As evening approached, I went to the purser's office on C-Deck. The head purser, a British man named Mr. McElroy, was standing at the window.

"Hello, can I help you?" McElroy inquired.

"I need someone's cabin number," I said.

"Certainly. Do you know the party's name?"

"Gregory. Anton Gregory."

"Ah, the gallery owner," McElroy said. He rifled through the passenger list that sat on his desk.

"As it happens, Mr. Gregory is on this deck," he said. "Cabin C-22."

"Thank you, sir."

Dinner would be served soon. I wondered if Anton left his room unlocked while he was in the dining room, as many of the first class passengers did, unthreatened by theft from their fellow aristocrats.

Don't be crazy, I told myself. *He'll catch you, just like Charles did.*

But I had no choice. I couldn't comprehend the cowardliness of letting Anton get away with selling the necklace. My real father had taught me better than that.

*   *   *

I noticed some of the first class passengers emerging from their rooms in evening wear, meandering toward D-Deck for the nightly social hour they called supper. I sat in the first class reception room and waited. As soon as I spotted Anton, I'd go back to his stateroom.

As the clock neared six, I saw Anton at the top of the stairs, black hair slicked back, arm-in-arm with a finely dressed blonde woman. He must have met her on board.

I moved quietly before Anton could see me.

C-Deck was empty. Most of the passengers were one deck below, eating dinner in the dining room. This was my only chance.

I stopped outside of stateroom C-22, checking in both directions to make sure no one was watching me. I heard a slight stir in the room across the hall, then nothing. It was silent.

I twisted the doorknob. There was no resistance. The door cracked open with ease, allowing me to peer into Anton's darkened stateroom.

I stepped inside and flipped the lights on.

The room, though small compared to my stateroom on B-Deck, seemed overwhelming. The bureau was in perfect order; the luggage was stacked neatly under the bed. Nothing grabbed my attention. There was no indication of where the necklace might be. Where did I look first?

I opened a drawer. I heard a door slam in the hallway, and the sound was nearly enough to make me jump out of my skin.

"I can't believe I'm doing this," I breathed to myself. I tried not to imagine what Anton would do if he caught me.

Underneath one of Anton's meticulously pressed shirts, I felt something. A notebook. I pulled it out and held it up to the light.

I knew exactly what it was before I opened it. On the cover was a black palm print against a white backdrop. *The Black Hand,* I thought, my heart pounding. This was the group of Serbian nationalists Anton was funding!

I flipped through it. Inside were pages and pages of names, addresses, and notes. Some of the notes were scrawled in a Slavic language. I had in my hands the membership list of a dangerous secret society.

I slipped the notebook into my pocket, feeling time tick away. I rummaged through the empty luggage, taking great pains to put everything back in its place.

I have to find that necklace before dinner ends! I thought, silently panicking.

Then I spotted something on Anton's dresser. It was a colorfully painted Russian nesting doll, the kind they'd sell at the World's Fair. It was also an unremarkable item, one that wouldn't catch the eye of a curious steward. It was a perfect hiding place.

I picked it up. As I suspected, something was inside…and it wasn't more wooden dolls. I heard a heavy *thud* as something rolled from side to side.

In one swift motion, I cracked open the doll and dropped the precious string of diamonds into my hand. My palms were so sweaty I nearly lost my grip.

I thought of what Charles had said to Mr. Rathbone: *Anton will sell the necklace for me. In the event the truth about the steel ever surfaces and Lake Erie Steel is ruined, I have insurance.*

"Not anymore, you slimy old man," I said to myself with a triumphant smile. And with that, I flipped off the lights and eased Anton's door closed, leaving the stateroom exactly as I'd found it.

*   *   *

Now I had to go and find Rudy. I'd committed his cabin number to my memory: A-14. I would give him Anton's notebook, figuring he had more use for it than I did.

My other dilemma was what to do with the necklace. It was vital to keep it out of Charles' hands, even though he'd find out sooner or later that I had stolen it back from Anton's room.

I found Rudy's stateroom just as dinner was ending.

"Rudy," I called, rapping on the door. "It's John Conkling."

I heard my knocks echoing inside the cabin. Although I was almost certain no one was inside, I tried again anyway out of desperation. I had to relieve myself of the notebook before Anton realized it was missing.

"Rudy?"

I was answered with more silence.

"Dammit," I cursed to myself, feeling Anton's notebook under my jacket. "What am I going to do with this?"

There was one person aboard who might know where I could find Rudy. I went back to the purser to get the LaRoe's stateroom number.

"She's a family friend," I quickly explained, trying to sound casual.

"Edith LaRoe and her daughter are on A-Deck," Purser McElroy told me. I committed the number to memory and hurried there, hoping to catch Faye returning from dinner.

Luckily, she answered on the first knock.

"Where were you tonight?" she asked. Faye looked pale and weary. Her expression was tense, as if she could sense trouble brewing. "Your stepfather wasn't happy that you were missing."

"Something more important came up," I said. "I need to talk to Rudy."

"He said I wouldn't be able to find him today," Faye said. "He's in hiding."

"What?" I responded, galled by such a statement. "It's a ship. Where could he possibly hide?"

"He has German associates aboard," she said. "That's all I know. Last night, he told me he was in danger, and to be careful who I trusted. The dark gentleman is onto him."

She was talking about Anton. I subconsciously tightened my grip on his notebook.

Faye's eyes grew sad. "I doubt I'll ever see him again when we land," she said. "He wasn't like the other men in first class. He told me jokes — bad ones, but they made me laugh. At night, he took me out to see the stars."

Her posture stiffened a bit. "I might even say I was falling in love with him," she told me. "But that would be pretty foolish, wouldn't it?"

"Faye, don't cry," I said. "I'm working with Rudy against Anton. He's not going to get away with hurting us. In fact, I need your help, too."

I handed her the notebook.

"Can you keep this for the time being?" I asked. "If Rudy comes back, please give it to him."

Faye's eyebrows furrowed in confusion as she examined the cover, with its ominous-looking black fist. "What is it?" she asked.

"Anton's the financier of an underground terrorist group," I said. "Rudy can use that notebook against him. It's incredibly valuable."

"I'll keep it safe with me," she agreed. "And John, if you see Rudy, can you tell him to please come to me?"

"Yes," I said. "I promise."

Now that the notebook was in safe hands, I had one more mission to complete. Unfortunately, it was one that had to wait until late tonight, when Charles was in a sound, liquor-induced sleep.

Seven

The clock was nearing eleven when I stepped out into the frigid night.

The Boat Deck was deserted, save for a lone crewman on the night watch. As I walked toward the stern, I spotted another lonely figure standing at the railing, head down. I recognized the dark curls and the long brocade skirt instantly.

"Mother!" I cried. "What are you doing out here alone?"

She didn't turn to look at me, although it was obvious she recognized my voice. "Not now, John."

I walked up to her and put my hand on her shoulder. Even in the darkness, I could see clearly that she was crying.

"Charles received a telegram," she said before I could ask. "He's in the smoking room, of course, but the steward brought it to our stateroom. He's to meet with his lawyer when we get to Cleveland. He wants a divorce."

I said nothing. I still didn't want to reveal the conversation I'd overheard in Mr. Rathbone's stateroom, although time was running out. I had to confront Charles and save Mother before the *Titanic* docked in New York.

"Why would he divorce me?" Mother wept. "I don't know if it's because I've given him no more children, or because of my ailment…" She wiped her eyes with the back of her hand.

"Or it's because of neither," I interrupted. "Mother, Charles is a bad man. I know it. Sadie knows it. You have to know that by now, too."

"But I need him," she said.

"No, you don't," I replied. "Bridget has a letter that will ruin him. If I have to, I'll turn it over to the newspapers myself."

"Besides, I'm your son. I'll always support you."

She hesitated, looking away with shame. "We're husband and wife in name only," she said. "Charles has had mistresses for years. Other men's wives, daughters of friends…the maids."

"Was Bridget one of them?" I asked.

"I don't know," she responded, weeping. "All I know is that he planned to fire her, and then she up and left one day. I was shocked. Sadie was so fond of her."

"And Charles didn't give you any clues about why she left?" I asked.

"No. He was very secretive about the whole affair," she said. "He was secretive about Lake Erie Steel as well. He thinks I'm stupid, but I knew he was in trouble, and that he had something to hide."

I shook my head, wishing I'd known all of this long ago.

"And in the meantime, he was becoming more and more entangled with Anton," Mother said. "When Charles and I went to his Gallery, he had dark men—Serbs—gathered downstairs, plotting. I heard a rumor they plan to assassinate the duke of Austria!" She gasped and widened her eyes at the memory. "That was when I knew I couldn't trust him. He was giving money to people called—"

"The Black Hand." I unwittingly completed the sentence for her, not thinking before I spoke it.

Mother turned to me open-mouthed. "How did you know that, John?"

"Don't worry about it," I replied. "Listen, Mother, you can't go back to Charles tonight. It's dangerous."

"I have nowhere else to go," she protested.

"Yes you do," I said. "I have someone to meet, but go to my room and wait for me."

There was no response.

"Do you promise to go to my stateroom?" I repeated. I was more insisting than asking.

She stared out at the ocean. Then, slowly, she nodded.

"I'll be back in an hour, maybe sooner," I said. "Lock the door and stay away from Charles. If you see him coming, run away. Is that clear?"

She nodded again.

"Go back inside," I said as I turned toward the second class stairs. "It's too cold for you to be out here all night."

The second class stairwell was eerily quiet. Occasionally I'd hear laughter, or a slamming door somewhere within the hallway. But as the clock passed eleven o'clock on a Sunday night, most of the passengers were retiring to bed.

The third class decks were more alive. Passengers wandered up and down Scotland Road. I listened to their conversations, hoping one of them might have word of Bridget.

"Hey, man, come up to the lounge!" one steerage man shouted to another. "We've got a poker tournament going. It should last the whole night long." Another man stumbled by, visibly drunk and trying not to trip over his well-worn boots.

Finally, I made it to cabin F-28 and knocked on the door. I could see through the cracks that the lights inside were still on.

Mary answered. "You again!" she said, before turning her head inside and whispering, "It's John Conkling."

Bridget appeared in the doorway. This time, she was wearing a long black coat, the embroidered shawl draped around her hair. She smelled like the cold ocean air, and her hair was wind-tossed.

"I've been looking for you," I said.

She stepped out in the hallway and shut the door behind her.

"What are you doing here? I don't have the letter," she said. She clutched the shawl tightly with one hand. "Jim has it still."

"I'm not here for the letter," I said. "I need to talk to you."

She stared up at me with fierce green eyes.

"You don't understand," she said. "I *can't* talk to you. Jim won't allow it. He heard what happened the other night, when we stood out on the deck for a long time, talking. He says I'm not to speak to you until we get the money, and never again after that. My brother's all I have."

"Please listen to me," I said. "You and Jim are in trouble, and so am I. Charles is dangerous."

Her glare intensified. "Is this all a trick?" she asked. "You sneak down here, saying you're doing Mr. Conkling's dirty work, and now you say you're afraid of him? You promised Jim the money. I told him he was wrong about you, and —"

She cut herself off suddenly, refusing to finish her sentence.

"And why do you call him 'Charles'?" she asked instead. "Is that some rich man's game you play?"

"I call him that because he's not my father," I replied.

"What?"

"He's not my father," I repeated. "My father died a decade ago. And he was nothing like Charles. My mother lost one husband, and now Charles is planning to divorce her and leave her with nothing."

Bridget squeezed her eyes shut for a moment as if she were in pain. Then she grabbed my coat sleeve. "Good God, come this way, will you?" she demanded.

We went up the same flight of stairs we had taken two nights ago to the third class deck. Bridget didn't talk until we stepped outside, with not a soul around to overhear us.

"I want to know why you're here," she said. "You know Jim has the letter, and you'll not be seeing it until he has the money in his hand. I tried to reason with him, but he would hear none of it."

"Charles isn't going to give you the money," I said, sucking in a deep breath. I might as well tell her now. "I overheard a conversation between him and his manservant. He said he's going to get that letter, even if he has to kill for it. I think he means it. He's already tried to poison my mother."

"He's already tried to *what?*"

"Please, I don't want you to panic," I continued. "I don't know what Charles has planned for you, but get word to Jim not to

101

meet with him under any circumstances. I'll warn Jim myself, if it comes to that."

"We have to tell him now," she said, her voice insistent.

"Do you know where he is?"

"He's been in the lounge all night with Patrick, and Brendan and Barry." She paused, remembering the way the boys had pummeled me on Friday. "Maybe I should go alone."

"I'll go with you. I'll tell him everything. I'm in the same danger from Charles that both of you are," I said. "I'm not what he hoped for, even though he desperately wanted a son."

"I'm surprised he didn't make one with another woman, then," Bridget said.

I straightened my back. I thought of what Mother had told me on the Boat Deck.

"Why did you run away from his house?" I asked. "Were you his mistress?"

"Good God, no," she replied. "But he tried. Oh, he tried. One night, while I was cleaning up after supper, he came up behind me and put his hands here." She placed her palms on her lower back. "…He tried to kiss me. But I wanted nothing to do with him, and I told him so. He cursed at me and called me nasty words. He told me I was ungrateful."

Bridget shook her head with revulsion.

"After that, he threatened to fire me," she said. "Jim is the one who told me I had to leave; told me not to let Mr. Conkling use me like that. Not even for a decent wage and a roof over my head." Her eyes glistened, and she hung her head for a moment.

At last, she said, "I knew you weren't his."

"Whose?"

"Mr. Conkling's," she replied. "I knew from your portraits you didn't look like him, not in the slightest. But it was something else, too, when I saw you coming down the stairs to the lounge. You're not like him." She looked up at me and loosened the shawl around her hair.

"And I never will be," I said.

I put his hand on her waist. I didn't think before I did it, but to my surprise, she didn't pull away. Instead, she tugged gently on my jacket to bring my face level with hers, and her lips grazed mine.

"What's this?"

Bridget and I spun around to find Jim standing on the deck, for once looking more shocked than angry. And for the first time, he was alone. Patrick and Barry were out of sight.

Jim was clutching a brown package in his left hand.

"Jim!" Bridget hissed, pulling away from me. "What are you doing here?"

He was flabbergasted. "I'm here because we were supposed to be meetin' here!" he exclaimed. "You convinced me to hand this over so you could get our cash."

"I don't have it," I said.

"What do you mean you don't have it?" He turned to Bridget. "What did I tell you? Conkling sent his boy down here to sweet-talk you and get the letter without sparing a dime for it. And now look at you. Are you kissing him? Bridie, you're a fool."

I put my hands in the air. "Please, Jim, don't get angry at her."

"Shut up," Jim snapped. "The deal's off. This letter will go to the New York papers as soon as we land." He waved the package around for me to see. "Bridie, come with me."

She froze.

"Bridie, get over here now," he repeated forcefully.

I grabbed Bridget around the waist as Jim stepped closer to us. For a moment I thought I felt the *Titanic* begin to turn. But it must have been my head spinning. If Charles didn't kill me first, I was sure Jim would be honored to do so.

"Get your filthy hands off of her!" Jim ordered. "Conkling, I'm warning you."

He reached into his pocket. When his hand emerged, I could see the moonlight glinting on the knife as he flipped the switchblade open.

"Stop!" Bridget shrieked.

As the cry escaped her mouth, the *Titanic* began to tremble and groan, as if we were running aground. I knew Bridget and Jim felt it, because they stopped talking, looking around for the source of the strange noise. Then, almost as soon as we'd noticed it, the ship began to vibrate. Jim's knife clattered on the deck.

"What the—"

All of a sudden, I saw a white mountain coming right for us, so massive it towered as high as the Boat Deck.

"Watch out!" I cried, jerking Bridget backward from the rail. She lost her footing.

Chunks of ice crashed onto the deck. The mountain sailed by and took the sickening grinding noise with it.

"Christ Almighty, that was an iceberg!" Jim exclaimed.

I remembered the ice notices Harold Bride, the wireless operator, had delivered to the captain that morning. Captain Smith had dismissed him. He even mentioned that Bruce Ismay wanted to increase our speed.

Within moments, the *Titanic* glided to a dead stop. The ship swayed in the ocean as the engines died. We had become accustomed to hearing the gentle hum of the ship, day in and day out, since we boarded. Now it was alarmingly quiet.

The door to the deck burst open. My heart jumped. *Charles! God, no!*

Instead, it was a steerage man standing in the doorway. "What was that?" he called. "We just felt a jolt up in the lounge. It knocked our beers clear off the table."

Jim waved his hand around at the deck. "Iceberg," he replied gruffly.

"Really, now?" the man called back. "Well that's a sight you don't see every day. I'll have to tell the boys to come out and have a look."

Bridget looked down at the chunks of ice around her boots.

"Why are we stopped?" she asked.

The steerage men began pouring out onto the deck, excited to see what had caused the jolt. They began kicking ice back and forth playfully. Some picked them up and threw it to each other, playing catch.

"Let's go," Jim said to Bridget a third time. "Conkling had his chance. The letter's ours now."

"So keep the letter," I said. "Give it to the papers if you want. I'm not working with my stepfather anymore, and Lake Erie Steel means nothing to me now."

"Is that the truth?" he said, staring at me skeptically.

"I have nothing to gain from lying."

"Hey Jim, how about some football?" another voice interrupted.

It was the redhead Patrick. He nudged a chunk of ice with his foot, watching it glide in

Jim's direction. Then he pointed at me. "Hey, what's that first class nancy-boy doing here?"

"Not now, Pat," Jim said impatiently. He turned back to Bridget. "I'm going back to my part of the ship to see what's going on," he said.

Then he pointed at me.

"And you," he said. "Walk her back to her room. And just in case you turn out to be a good liar, I'm taking this." He held up the envelope.

"Yes," I said quietly. A steward was on the deck now, corralling the men back inside. We followed them toward the doors.

"I'll come back to the stern to find you," Jim said to Bridget at the top of the third class stairwell. He put his hands on her shoulders and looked her in the eye. "Whatever the crew tell you to do, do it. Don't wait. If they send you up top, go."

Bridget bit her lip and nodded. Then they parted ways.

There was no commotion on F-Deck. In fact, all of the doors were shut. If any of the women had noticed the jolt, it wasn't enough to stir them from bed.

Mary and Brendan were coming down the hallway, grinning and looking lighthearted.

"Bridget!" Mary called. "Where did you go?"

"Don't ask," Bridget replied sullenly.

"Do you know why we're stopped?"

107

"Well, we just brushed by an iceberg," Bridget replied. "The deck's covered in ice. I don't know why they killed the engines, though."

Both of the girls looked up at me for reassurance.

"They're probably making sure everything is in order down below before we keep going," I said, having no idea whether it was true.

A stern-faced woman rounded the corner. Bridget and Mary cringed.

"Oh Lord, here comes the matron," Mary muttered. "We better get movin'."

The matron began pounding on doors, flinging open the ones that were unlocked. "Everybody up!" she called inside the rooms. "Everyone get up and put your lifebelts on."

"Lifebelts!" Mary exclaimed. "Those big ugly white things? What use do we have for those, now?"

Sleepy women began stumbling into the hallway in nightgowns. Some chattered back and forth confusedly to each other, unable to understand the orders.

"Girls, get your lifebelts on," the matron said, then looked at Brendan and me. "And what are you doing here at midnight? You know the rules. Now get back to your rooms before I kick you down there!"

"Miss Wallis, what's going on?" Bridget asked.

"Just get your lifebelt on, Miss Bridget."

"But why?" Bridget persisted. "Why are we stopped?"

"I don't know," the matron repeated stubbornly. "I am simply relaying captain's orders. Now do as I say and wait for instructions from the crew." She pounded on the next door.

For the first time since I met her, Mary's face was somber.

"I have to find my brother," she said. "I don't want to get separated from him."

"The boys went back to the bow to get their luggage," I told her. "They're coming right back. Everything will be fine, Mary. I promise."

"How do you know?"

"I met the designer of the ship, Thomas Andrews," I said. "He explained to me how the watertight compartments worked. We're not going to sink."

"...He's Irish, by the way," I added, and the girls smiled a little, looking relieved.

Some of the women were filing out into the hallway with their White Star lifebelts, fussing with straps, moving the cumbersome sheets of cork back and forth.

"I'll help you with yours," I said to Bridget. We entered the room she shared with Mary and the two Scandinavian girls, who were sitting wide-eyed in bed. I dug the lifebelts out from under the bunks. I pulled it down over Bridget's head and tied the straps. Then I motioned to the Scandinavian girls, offering help.

"Look at these ugly things!" Mary cried. "I look like a fat seagull. How long do we have to wear them?"

"Just leave it on until the crewmen say otherwise," I said. "It shouldn't be long."

Brendan took Mary's hand. "I best be leaving here, too, before the matron comes back," he said. He gave her a kiss before he left.

"Me and Pat's tickets are in here somewhere," Mary said, rooting around under her bunk. "I'm sure they'll want 'em if we get sent up top. And the suitcase..."

As Mary talked to herself, I pulled Bridget into the hallway.

"What are you doing?" she whispered. "I have to help Mary. Something serious is going on and she doesn't know it."

"Come up top with me," I said.

"What?"

"Come up top with me to first class," I repeated. "I have my ticket in my pocket. The lift attendants won't question it. If there's an emergency, you'll be safer there than down here."

We watched a woman struggling to strap lifebelts over her children's pajamas. They fussed and cried at the indignity of being awake at this hour, captain's orders or not.

"I can't," Bridget finally said.

"We can't stay down here," I persisted. "We have to get through the gates while there's still time. If there's a real emergency, they could forget all about coming back to let us out."

"Then you go and I'll stay," she insisted. "My brother told me to wait here while he gets our things, and then he'll be back. Jim honors his promises."

I let out a deep breath. I could see that Bridget's boots were planted firmly. She didn't rock or waver, the way I'd seen her do when she was nervous. She wasn't going anywhere.

"I'll come back for you," I said. "After I find my mother and Sadie, I'll make my way down here and bring you up to the Boat Deck. Jim can come, too."

"Alright."

"One more thing," I said. "Can you hold onto this for me?"

I pulled out Mother's necklace and slipped it into her pocket. It was more dangerous for Charles and Anton to catch me with it than to leave it with Bridget.

She gasped when she saw it.

"It's Mrs. Conkling's necklace!" she exclaimed. "John, I can't take this!"

"Hold onto it, just for a while," I said. "Consider it a promise that I'll be back."

Then I turned and walked away. I knew the longer I stood there, the harder it would be to leave her.

*   *   *

A crewman was locking the gate at the top of the stairs.

"Hey!" I yelled. "Let me through."

"Stay down there," the crewman barked. "I have orders to keep these gates locked until the officers say otherwise."

"I'm first class!" I argued.

"Sure you are. Now go back downstairs and put your lifebelt on."

I dug frantically in my jacket pocket until I felt the piece of paper that had been there since Southampton.

"I have a first class ticket," I said, thrusting my hand through the gate. "My name's John Conkling and my stepfather owns Lake Erie Steel. He put the steel in this ship. Now let me through before it costs you your job!" I didn't sound like myself as I said it.

The sailor ripped the ticket from my hand and glanced at it.

"You can't go back down once I lock this gate behind you," the sailor growled. "What are you doing here, anyway? You're to report to the Boat Deck in your lifebelt immediately."

I thought of Bridget. I put one foot behind me, torn between going back to F-Deck and finding Mother and Sadie. If the *Titanic* was in danger, I had to get to them before Charles did.

"Alright, let me through," I said, knowing I had to somehow find my way back down again.

*　　　*　　　*

The elevators were still running. The lift attendant smiled, as he always did, giving no indication that anything was amiss.

"Where to, sir?" he asked as I stepped on.

"A-Deck."

"You're my last passenger, I'm afraid," the attendant said. "I've been ordered to close the lifts for the night. Evidently, we've dropped a propeller blade."

I didn't bother telling him about the iceberg. A few seconds later I stepped onto A-Deck, where a few passengers milled around under the Grand Staircase, no lifebelts in sight. Not one of them looked alarmed.

I spotted Max Seligman standing near the railing and rushed up to him.

"Max," I said. "What have they told you?"

"Not much," he said. "I was in the smoking room playing blackjack when we stopped. They're saying we're stuck in an ice field for the night."

"It's only a minor delay, gentlemen," a steward said as he passed by. "We should be underway shortly."

I turned to Max.

"They're not telling us the truth," I said. "I think we've hit an iceberg. I saw it when I was out on the deck."

"A berg?" Max repeated, sounding more intrigued than worried. "Well, I'm not surprised. I overheard one of the rich guys talking to Ismay at dinner. They decided to light the last four boilers and plow full speed ahead, despite all the ice warnings."

He shook his head. "Oh, speak of the devil," he said.

Bruce Ismay and Thomas Andrews were rushing through the Grand Staircase. Andews was carrying a blueprint of the ship, clutching it so tightly his knuckles were white.

"The mailroom's gone," I heard him say. "They're already dragging sacks of mail up the stairs to keep it out of the water. I hope the pumps can buy us a little time."

Max looked at me incredulously. "This ship can't sink," he said. "What about the watertight doors and the pumps? Maybe they're already running them and that's why we're stopped."

"Maybe," I replied. "But I'm going to go see what's going on."

"Me, too," Max said. "I'm sure I'll see you around later, John. Stop by the smoking room if you get a chance."

Some of the first class passengers on B-Deck had come out of their rooms by now.

"Excuse me, sir, what's going on?" one lady, clad in a nightgown and a fur overcoat, asked a steward from her doorway. "I heard a grinding noise."

"There are some minor problems in the engine room," the steward replied. "But as a precaution, the captain has requested that everyone put their lifebelts on."

The engine room. An ice field. A dropped propeller blade. Why wouldn't they tell anyone about the iceberg?

I could only guess that the damage was so great, they were simply trying to ward off the panic.

"It'll take a lot more than engine problems to get me out of bed on a Sunday night," one man said grumpily. He shut his door behind him.

I pounded on the door to Mother and Charles' stateroom. There was no answer.

"Mother? Are you in there?" I called.

Silence.

Mr. Bowen was coming down the hallway. "Mr. Conkling, do you need assistance with your lifebelt?" he asked.

"I can manage. Have you seen my parents tonight?"

"The elder Mr. Conkling was headed to the smoking room last I saw him," Mr. Bowen said. "But I believe that room will be closed during this delay."

"But you haven't seen my mother?" I pressed.

"No sir, not since they were going to dinner."

I went to the next door, Celia and Sadie's room. Celia answered, looking irritated with the commotion. She squinted at me.

"What's going on?" she asked. "It's past midnight."

"Get your lifebelt on and come outside," I said impatiently. "Put Sadie's on, too."

"But she's fast asleep," she said.

"It's captain's orders."

Sadie sat up in her bed. "Johnny?" she said, rubbing her eyes. "Where's Mommy?"

"That's a good question," I said, looking at Celia. "Have you seen her or Charles? Because the steward hasn't."

"I assume she's sleeping."

I stepped into the room and found the two lifebelts inside the closet.

"Celia, please get Sadie dressed," I said. "If the stewards request it, go up top to the Boat Deck. Follow their orders and dress warmly. I'll come back to check on you after I find my mother."

"Don't be absurd," Celia scoffed. "A seven-year-old outside at this hour? In this cold?" She turned to my sister. "Sadie, go back to sleep, dear."

"You had better follow orders," I warned her.

I knocked on Mother's door once again.

"Mother, please wake up," I called. "We have to go up top." But I had a sinking feeling that she wasn't inside the room. The last time I'd seen her, she was alone on the Boat Deck. Maybe she'd finally given into her constant sadness and climbed over the rail.

Or maybe Charles had come across her when no one else was watching.

I raced out to the first class staircase, where more passengers were congregating, exchanging pleasantries and comments on the peculiar events unfolding in front of them.

"I hear it's a lifeboat drill," one woman said. "How dreadful to do it so late on a Sunday night! I'll think twice before sailing with White Star again."

"Not only that, but it's cold as the Dickens outside," her husband added.

I started to think about the temperature. Every winter in Cleveland, someone fell through the ice out on the lake. Sometimes their bodies washed ashore in spring, sometimes not. But they never survived long enough for anyone to rescue them.

If that water is freezing, these lifebelts won't buy us more than twenty minutes of life, I realized. I decided not to put mine on. I was a strong swimmer, and what would a lifebelt do for me in thirty-degree water?

It was time to go back to the Boat Deck to see if Mother was still there. Once I found her, I'd get her, Sadie, and Celia into a boat. Then I'd go back for Bridget.

It was now half past midnight. Less than an hour had passed since the collision, and the deck was already beginning to tilt. I was mindful of the unevenness as I walked up the stairs, grasping the railing and being careful not to fall.

There was no longer any doubt about the *Titanic*'s fate. We were going down by the bow, and fast.

*   *   *

People were slowly trickling out onto the Boat Deck. I followed them, even though the cold felt like needles stinging my face.

The smokestacks were letting off a long, low, continuous scream. The deck crew scrambled about, ripping the canvas covers off the lifeboats.

"Swing these boats over!" a burly sailor yelled. The brand new davits groaned as the ropes were cranked outward, positioning the boats over the water.

All of a sudden the smokestacks stopped bellowing. The passengers fell silent, too, caught off guard by the sudden quiet.

"Attention, please," a man in a navy blue White Star jacket and cap shouted. It was Officer Murdoch, a man I saw on deck occasionally, talking with Captain Smith. "Attention!"

The passengers stood listening, some looking confused, others bored. But mostly, they looked cold, stomping their feet and rubbing gloved hands together to stay warm. I thought again about the freezing water. If a rescue ship didn't reach us in time, half the people standing here would be plunged into it along with the ship.

"For the time being, I am loading these boats with women and children," Murdoch said. "Please step toward me. This way, please."

The crowd hesitated, holding a collective breath. Husbands and wives looked at each other. The woman next to me, holding a child against the hump of her lifebelt, stared up at the man beside her.

"Not without you," she said.

"We have to listen to officers," he said, rubbing her shoulders to comfort her. "You heard Mr. Murdoch. It's women and children first, but only for the time being. There will be plenty of boats left over." He motioned toward the row of empty lifeboats on the first class deck.

Her face was still clouded with doubt. But with her husband's arm around her, she stepped forward slowly, handing the child to Murdoch before he helped her step into the boat.

"Don't worry," another man told his wife as she approached the lifeboat. "As soon as they get this mess sorted out, the sailors will row back to the ship. You'll be aboard again before breakfast!"

"Are there any more women and children?" Murdoch bellowed out, his breath freezing in the air. A man stepped forward, hand-in-hand with a young girl. Murdoch scanned him up and down. "Women and children first," he repeated firmly, narrowing his eyes.

The boat was still half empty, but the passengers hung back.

"No way am I getting into that little boat," one woman declared stubbornly. "I get horribly seasick. In fact, I'd like nothing more than to go back to bed." She and her husband turned back inside, where it was warm.

"Alright, men can step aboard now," Murdoch said, looking discouraged. Much to the relief of their wives, a few of the husbands climbed into the boat.

Murdoch turned to the crewmen manning the davits. "That's all for this one," he said. "Lower away."

The boat jerked downward unevenly — front end first, then back. Some of the women aboard screamed and clutched the edges.

"Steady!" Murdoch barked. "You'll dump them all into the sea."

I leaned over the railing and tried to count the boat's occupants as it lowered. Twenty-five or so, in a boat built for almost seventy. Looking forward, I could see the bow of the *Titanic* dipping lower into the ocean, the still-burning lights inside casting an eerie green glow onto the surface of the water.

Fireworks exploded overhead, lighting up the black horizon for a brief moment. The passengers gasped — some with awe, others with confusion.

"What the hell is going on?" a man asked as the smoldering white lights fizzled. "Those look like distress rockets. Surely this can't be serious."

The ship's orchestra had set up on the Boat Deck. They played a loud, lively tune as the crewmen began to load the next boat, cajoling the women to step aboard with little success. This boat, too, was half-empty.

There was no time to waste. I had to get Sadie into a boat, even if she had to go without Mother. I went back inside, where even more passengers were waiting in the

Grand Staircase. Stewards milled in and out with trays of drinks. "The smoking room is now open for the night, gentlemen," one of the stewards said. "The blackjack tables are open as well. Would you care for a cocktail?"

They're trying to keep us calm, I realized as I took the stairs to B-Deck.

I found Celia and Sadie in their stateroom, where they had reluctantly dressed for the cold. Sadie was wearing an odd ensemble of a winter coat, mittens, and stockings under her nightgown.

"I thought it would be easier to get her back into bed later," Celia explained.

"Celia, we're not going back to bed," I said. "The ship's sinking. They're already launching the lifeboats. I'm going to get you and Sadie into one before they're all gone."

They both stared at me, round-eyed. For the first time in months, Sadie didn't whine or argue with me. I helped them both into their lifebelts, fastening the straps snugly — even though I knew, in this cold, it wouldn't make much difference.

"What about the luggage?" Celia asked.

"Leave it," I said. "There's not enough room for all the people aboard this ship, let alone their suitcases."

"Can I bring my doll?" Sadie asked.

"Yes, Sadie."

"Are you coming in the boat with us?"

I looked down at her, unsure of what to say. "I'll be in a different boat," I lied. "So will Mommy."

The atmosphere in the Grand Staircase was more urgent now. "Can you believe this?" a man said to no one in particular, sounding agitated. "No organization, no plan of attack!"

"Don't worry," another man replied. "I heard the *Titanic* can't possibly founder in less than eight hours. Another ship will be here to take us on long before that."

Ahead of me, I spotted a blonde bun. Faye and Mrs. LaRoe were standing in the thick of the crowd, looking overwhelmed by the scene.

"If you've come to get me to leave, I'm not going," Faye said before I could get a word in.

"Please, Faye. I know you're sad about Rudy, but what good will it do to wait for him?" I asked. "The ship is sinking fast. You need to get to a lifeboat while they're still here."

"Not without him."

"What about your mother?" I persisted. "With your father gone, you're all she has left."

Faye gazed down at her feet and nodded reluctantly. She still looked dejected, as she had this evening, when it became clear she wouldn't see Rudy.

"I still have the notebook," she said.

"Good. Hold onto it until you see Rudy again," I replied, although that might never happen. "Now let's get going."

I led Celia, Sadie, and the LaRoes up the staircase to the port side of the Boat Deck, where a group of first class passengers was clustered around a lifeboat. Captain Smith was standing before it, bellowing into a megaphone as he herded women aboard.

"Any more ladies?" Captain Smith asked. There were twenty aboard, at the most.

"Right here," I called out, then said to all four of them, "Ladies, are you ready?"

Faye nodded bravely. She took Captain Smith's hand and stepped over the gap between the deck and the boat, being careful not to rock it. Then Mrs. LaRoe and Celia climbed in.

I was left holding Sadie.

"Are you ready to get into the boat?" I asked her. "Celia will take care of you."

"I want to stay here with you," she said.

"I have to get into a different boat later," I told her again. "But for now, you have to go with Celia. Be a big girl and don't cry."

Sadie nodded quietly.

"This way, Miss Conkling," Captain Smith said with a forced smile. He lifted Sadie over the gap and dropped her into the boat.

"That's all, then?" Smith asked as he scanned the crowd of men remaining on the deck. "Lower this boat."

I could barely stand to watch it drop away. "Goodbye, Johnny," Sadie called up to me over the loud groan of the davits, her tiny face bewildered. At least she didn't cry.

"Goodbye, Sadie," I said. "See you tomorrow!"

As the boat descended past A-Deck, I spotted the top of a familiar head, standing alone on the promenade.

"There he is!" I cried to myself, as I raced down the stairs to confront him.

Charles was smoking a cigarette and watching the boats launch, looking totally calm.

"Where's Mother?" I demanded.

"I haven't seen her all night," Charles said with a smirk. "But I do think she went up to the Boat Deck to hide from me. I think you know that as well as I do."

"I'm tired of playing your little games," I shot back. "Do you feel that slant under your feet? We're sinking. The lifeboats are for women and children only. Neither one of us is leaving this ship, so you might as well tell me where she is."

Charles ignored me. Instead, he reached into his pocket and pulled out his pack of cigarettes.

"Care for a smoke, John?" he asked. At that moment a low, loud groan emanated from the lower decks. "The evening's last, it would seem."

I could almost feel the tilt of the ship growing steeper by the moment. Although I never smoked, I reached for the cigarette.

Charles pulled out his pistol and aimed it at my stomach.

"Where's the necklace?" he demanded.

"I don't have it," I replied honestly, staring at the barrel of the gun.

"I know you took it from Anton's stateroom," he said. "I already searched your cabin while you were down below again, cavorting with that Irish tart. What did you do with it?"

"Maybe you shouldn't have entrusted it to a man who funnels money to anarchists."

Charles thrust his hands into my pockets, pressing the gun into me. He grew enraged as he came up empty-handed.

"Where is it?!"

Just then a crewman rounded the corner.

"What's going on here?" he barked. "This is no time for fighting. Now go up to the Boat Deck before I throw you both overboard!" A group of crewmen followed behind him, picking up deck chairs and hurling them overboard.

I shuddered at the prospect of using them to float.

Charles stuffed his pistol back inside his jacket. "Well, I suppose it doesn't matter where the necklace is now, does it?" he said. "As you might have guessed, I have a backup plan."

Charles took one last puff of his cigarette and pitched it into the sea.

"But I doubt you have a plan," he said. "You should go up top and see if you can still pass for a boy, rather than a man."

"I would never take a seat from a woman."

Charles laughed scornfully. "Enjoy the bottom of the ocean, John."

And with that, he disappeared up the stairs to the Boat Deck.

Eight

The crowd of first class men around me was calm, but serious, even as the band tried to keep our spirits up with a cheerful ragtime tune.

Captain Smith was still calling out orders with his megaphone, convincing women to leave their husbands and get into the next lifeboat. This one was slightly fuller than Sadie's boat — thirty women aboard, plus a few sailors to man the oars.

"Are there any more women?" Captain Smith called, his voice growing more and more anxious. "You, ma'am. Step this way."

I looked over my shoulder. He was talking to the Straus couple, the elderly owners of Macy's.

Mrs. Straus shook her head and stepped back, clasping Mr. Straus's hand. There was a tone of finality in the old woman's voice. "We have been living together for many years," she said to him, "and where you go, I go."

He gazed into her eyes for a long moment, as if he was debating whether to argue with her. Finally, he nodded, and they walked away from the boat, hand-in-hand.

At least people are starting to accept that we're sinking, I thought grimly.

"These boats are all two-thirds empty," a crewman said to Captain Smith. "What gives?"

The captain lifted his megaphone and turned outward to the sea.

"Boat six," he bellowed. "Row back to the ship!"

It was Sadie's boat. If they heard Captain Smith at all, they were ignoring his orders. Now that they were safely off the ship, what sense did it make to risk being swamped by terror-stricken swimmers?

"Boat six," Captain Smith ordered again, "Return to the ship to take on more passengers!"

But the crewmen kept on rowing until they faded into the darkness, visible only by a single lantern.

*   *   *

I wondered how far the sea had risen since we'd hit the iceberg. Surely the third class men's cabins were underwater by now, their few possessions swept into the ocean. The crew had probably pushed them back into the stern with the women.

It was time to go back to Bridget, as I'd promised.

I hurried toward the stern of the ship, past the crowds of second class passengers that were now gathering around the lifeboats.

"Swing these boats out!" one crewman called to another, as the passengers looked on anxiously.

"Excuse me, sir," I said, "where would the stewards take the third class passengers?"

"They'll board the boats from the gangway doors," he said.

I peered over the railing at the nearly seventy-foot drop to the water. "The gangway doors are shut," I said.

The crewman waved me away. "I don't have time for this," he said, irritated. "I've been ordered to prepare these boats for launch, that's all I know."

I wondered if Bridget and the other steerage passengers were still waiting behind the locked gates. The lifeboats at the front end of the ship were mostly gone, half-filled with first class passengers; I could see their lanterns scattered around in the distance. The boats at the stern were already surrounded by second class passengers waiting to board.

If the gates were still locked, the steerage passengers didn't stand a chance.

With the lifts closed down, I would have to take the staircase to E-Deck. I went against the flow of passengers, running down flights of steps as everyone else swarmed the Boat Deck. I ignored a steward who commanded me to turn around. There were, at most, eight lifeboats left. I was determined to get Bridget to one of them.

Just like the first night I'd been down here, I could hear the steerage passengers before I could see them. But this time, it wasn't the sound of merriment—it was fear. I immediately recognized Jim's voice.

"Good God, man, would you open up the gate and let the girls through!" he was shouting. "You can't keep them and their babes down here!"

Standing in front of the cast-iron gate was a man in a White Star Line uniform. On the other side was a crowd of Irish immigrants waiting on the stairs.

"You can't go up these stairs. It's the law," the crewman insisted. "Now, go back to the gangway door like I told you!"

"The gangway doors are shut," I said to him.

"Who are you and what are you doing down here?" he snarled. "Get up to the Boat Deck! It's *captain's* orders!"

"The boats are going fast," I replied. "At least open the gate and let the women and children have a chance."

"You don't understand," he replied. "If I let them through, the men will storm the boats. Look at how out-of-control they are already. I can't be responsible for a fiasco like that."

Bridget appeared at the top of the stairs beside Jim, her face white.

"John!" she cried. "We have to get out of here. When the boys went back to their cabins, the water was up to their shins." She glowered at the crewman.

"Unlock the gate," I told him again. "There are women and children down there."

He looked at me, then back at the crowd of frantic steerage passengers.

"Fine," he said. "But women and children only!" With one hand, he produced his keys—with the other, a pistol.

"Let John take you to a boat," Jim said to Bridget. He shot me a look, letting me know he was entrusting his sister to me. "Oh, and take this, Conkling."

Through the gate, he passed me the envelope with the letter.

"Thanks," I said, and wadded it up in my pocket. What difference did it make now, anyway? Jim and I both knew we weren't stepping foot in a lifeboat tonight.

The crewman inched the gate open just wide enough for Jim to push Bridget to the other side, before she had a chance to argue about leaving him.

"Bridget!" Mary called, pushing her way to the top of the stairs. "I'm going with you!"

The crewman grabbed Mary's arm and pulled her through. A rush of women followed. Men passed frightened children up the stairs until they could be shoved through, along with their mothers. A young man, about Jim's age, tried to shoulder his way out.

"I said no men!" the crewman shouted, thrusting his pistol into their faces. "Get back! Get back, I said!"

He slammed the gate shut on a gaggle of wild-eyed passengers. He frantically turned the key in the lock as they pushed forward, threatening to break it down.

We ran. The screams of the men faded into the background as we fled for the second class stairs. These decks looked like ghost towns that had been suddenly abandoned. Stateroom doors stood half-open, and forgotten luggage was strewn around the hallways.

"What's going to happen to the boys?" Bridget asked me. "They can't just leave them down there."

"I don't know," I replied, choosing to be honest with her. "The sailors loading the lifeboats are giving priority to the women and children."

"No way am I gettin' in one of those boats!" Mary said. "I'm from County Roscommon, for God's sake. I've never been in an open boat in my life."

"I'm from County Galway and I'm still not getting in," Bridget retorted.

"Well, we have some time," Mary said. "Everyone says we can't sink."

The deck was humming with activity. I could barely see the lifeboats through the crowd of passengers. As the *Titanic's* bow dipped lower into the ocean, people were migrating here, toward the stern.

I guided Bridget and Mary toward the boats, bumping into other passengers as the crowd tried to move about in the awkward lifebelts. I was thankful not to be wearing one.

"Get out of here, you coward!" I heard someone shout.

I pressed forward to see what was going on. It was Officer Lightoller, one of the senior officers on the *Titanic*, and the young Officer Lowe, tangling with a teenage boy who'd jumped into a lifeboat. Lowe grabbed the boy around the collar and dragged him to his feet.

"I give you ten seconds to get back on that ship before I blow your brains out!" Officer Lowe threatened, aiming his pistol at the boy's head.

A little girl in the boat grabbed the sleeve of Lowe's blue jacket. "Oh, Mr. Man," she begged, "please don't shoot him!" The women in the boat whimpered with fear.

Lowe and Lightoller both laughed a little.

"Come on," Lowe said to the stowaway. "Be a man. We've got women and children to save here."

The boy gave in and stepped onto the deck without a fight.

"Women and children, this way," Lightoller commanded, by now picking up women indiscriminately and chucking them into the boat, ignoring their protests. "We've no time to waste."

Mary turned to Bridget. "Should we get in?"

"Yes," I replied. "Both of you."

Bridget took a step backward. "Not me," she said forcefully. "I told you three times, I'm not going."

Mary was looking around the deck, taking in the chaos. She stared down at her feet for a few lingering seconds, noting the angle of the deck.

"Look at that slant," she remarked soberly. "It wasn't true what they said about the *Titanic* being unsinkable, was it?"

I didn't respond. I felt a rush of guilt for assuring the girls we were safe just two hours ago.

"That's all for this boat," Officer Lightoller called over the commotion. "Lower away!"

"Wait!" Mary yelled out. She flailed her arms in the air to get the officers' attention.

She turned around and gave Bridget a quick embrace. "I'm getting in," she said. "I'm so sorry, Bridget."

There was no time for words. Lightoller grabbed Mary and heaved her over the gap between the ship and the lifeboat. The *Titanic* was starting to list, leaning toward port.

"Mr. Lowe, man this boat," Lightoller said, and the younger officer stepped in. The ropes began creaking away in the davits.

"Bridget," Mary called up to us, "Tell Pat my lifeboat number!"

"I will, I promise!"

I didn't know how or when we would see Mary's brother again, but just in case, I remembered the number: fourteen.

There was a crowd of men standing around the davits, leering down at Mary's descending boat. I could see in their faces that they were thinking about defying the officers and jumping in. If they did, they would rock the boat hard enough to throw all the women overboard. Lowe stood inside the boat, brandishing his gun at the passengers on the deck.

"Get away from the lines!" he demanded, glaring at the passengers as if they were a pack of rabid dogs waiting to pounce.

A young dark-haired man jumped. I heard the terrified screams of the women and children as the boat swung wildly.

"Get out of here!" Lowe shouted, ejecting him with all his might.

The screams were quickly followed by three loud *cracks* as Lowe fired his pistol into the air. A gang of men pulled the stowaway aboard and surrounded him, driving their fists into his face over and over again.

"The next man who jumps gets a bullet in him," Lowe pronounced.

"Is anyone hurt?" a crewman called out. As far as I could see, no one had been hit by Lowe's bullets—but the shots had nevertheless sent terror rippling through the crowd.

"Everything's turning to madness," Bridget said. "Let's get out of here."

We rounded the stern of the ship, where another lifeboat was launching. I couldn't see any more boats on deck, only their empty lines. I was running out of time to get Bridget off the ship…and to find Mother. I wondered if she'd been put into a boat already. Maybe she was rowing away from the foundering *Titanic*—and from Charles.

But I had a gut feeling she wasn't safe.

"Are there any more boats left after this one?" I asked a sailor.

"Not here," he replied, "but there are a few left all the way forward, in first class."

The lifeboat in front of us was packed to capacity. As I watched it lower, I silently prayed that the wooden hull of the boat wouldn't splinter. It was the only thing between these seventy women and children and the dark, freezing sea.

As the boat neared the water, screams rang out from below.

"Stop lowering number fifteen!" a crewman's voice shouted, although nobody on deck was paying attention.

I leaned over the railing and saw that lifeboat fifteen was descending directly on top of another boat, so close the passengers could touch the bottom of it.

"The boats are about to collide!" I cried. At that moment, the first lifeboat broke away, pulling clear of number 15 just in time. One of the oarsmen had cut the ropes with a pocketknife.

"Let's go forward," I said to Bridget.

Before she could respond, there was more commotion on the deck.

"You're not allowed up here!" a crewman barked. "Get back, before I shoot you all like dogs!"

A mob of men was storming the gate between the third class deck and the Boat Deck. The crewmen threatened, waved pistols in the air, and shoved; the steerage men shoved back. One tumbled down the stairs, and the others hoisted him up, helping him over the gate. There was no stopping them now. The only thing on their minds was survival.

"Conkling, give me a hand!"

I looked up to find Jim and his friends climbing up a crane from the steerage deck. I grabbed his arm, and he dropped several feet to the deck.

"Bridie, I thought you'd be long gone!" Jim said, regaining his balance. He glared at me.

"There are a few boats left in the bow," I told him. "I can take her there."

"No," Bridget said to Jim. "I told you, I'd rather die than be alone in the world."

"Hush, now," Jim said. "There's no room for men like me in those boats. The boys and I will try our luck back here, in the stern."

"You have to promise me you'll save yourself, Jim," Bridget said.

"You know I don't go down without a fight." He pointed to the crane, indicating how far he had climbed just to reach the Boat Deck.

"Let's go," I said, and we ran down the deck, being careful not to lose our footing on the steepening slant.

The only remaining boat on the starboard side was beginning to lower. "Hey!" I shouted, trying to get the officer's attention. "She has to get in that boat!"

"This one's full," Officer Murdoch replied. "There are some left on the port side; you'll have to take her over there."

I looked over the railing at the descending boat, wondering if Bridget could jump in. It was filled with an odd mix of first and third class women, oarsmen…and, huddled in the corner, Bruce Ismay, the president of the White Star Line. The man who had ordered the *Titanic*'s officers to charge ahead at full speed was saving himself.

"Coward," I said to myself with disgust, as another distress rocket exploded overhead.

"Where did everyone go?" Murdoch asked. "They're all moving toward the stern. We need to load those last few boats on the port side."

"Officer Murdoch, how much time do we have?" I asked.

We both looked toward the sinking bow. The red lights of the *Titanic*'s mast still burned.

"An hour, if we're lucky," Murdoch replied. "Those few boats on the port side aren't prepared to launch yet. But when they are, make sure your lady friend is ready and waiting. There are probably more than a thousand people still on board."

"Thank you, sir," I said.

*   *   *

We went to the first class smoking room, where at least it was still warm and dry.

It was a madhouse. Men dressed in eveningwear still played cards, joking and laughing, trying to ignore the grotesque slant of the tables in front of them. A smoking room attendant was still passing out drinks.

"Would you like one, good sir? It's on the house," he said to me, then looked at Bridget. "For all classes, and ladies too."

If this were a normal night aboard the *Titanic*, I would have said no. Instead I accepted and drank it down, fast. To my surprise, Bridget did, too.

"I might as well," she said to me. "It could be our last."

I spotted Max across the room, playing blackjack at the French card dealer's table.

"Hey!" he exclaimed when he saw me, looking red-faced and excitable. "Crazy night, huh?"

Two firemen ran by, stuffing their pockets with bottles of liquor. They drank a few slugs from a flask as they passed our table.

"What do you think you're doing?" a steward asked. "That whiskey isn't yours!"

"Ah, shut up, old boy. We deserve to have our share," one of them said. "After we drink, it's down we go. Down to Davy Jones' locker."

Davy Jones' locker. According to maritime legend, it was the final resting place of dead sailors. I felt my stomach turn.

"Have you seen my mother at all tonight?" I asked Max.

"No, I haven't," he replied. "But I did see your stepfather prowling around here a while ago."

The *Titanic* lurched downward, letting out a giant, hideous groan. Drinks slid off the card tables. The men reached for anything they could grasp, and for the first time, I saw terror in their faces. I held on to Bridget.

"Time to wrap this game up and head for the Boat Deck," Max said to his tablemates. "It's been a good night, gentlemen."

He turned to me. "You know who else I haven't seen at all tonight?" he said. "That creep Gregory. I'm surprised he didn't try to bribe his way into a lifeboat."

"Anton Gregory?" Bridget said.

"You know him?"

"I met him at Mr. Conkling's house," she replied. "He was a cagey sort, always looking like he was up to no good. I thought he had ill will toward Mrs. Conkling."

All of a sudden, it dawned on me.

"Max, will you take Bridget to a lifeboat?" I asked.

"What?" Bridget stammered. "Where are you going?"

"I think I know where my mother is," I said.

"In fact, I'm *sure* I know where she is."

"Is that right?" Max said. "Well, do what you have to do."

He squeezed my shoulder a few times and tried to smile. "And if I don't see you again, it was great getting to know you, John," he said, then fell quiet.

"Good luck, Max," I said. "I won't forget you." This time, he managed a real smile.

Bridget followed me out of the smoking room. "You didn't really think I would go with your friend, did you?" she said. "I'm going with you."

I had learned by now not to argue with her.

"I was fond of Mrs. Conkling. She was good to me," Bridget said. "So let's go now; I'll help you save her."

"We have to go all the way to C-Deck," I told Bridget as we raced down the deserted first class staircase. I braced myself for a rising flood on our way down. There was no telling how far the water had risen, but I had to try to save Mother.

If my instincts were right, she was in terrible danger.

"Is this first class we're in?" Bridget said, looking around the ornate hallway, at the oak carvings and chandeliers. "It's so beautiful."

A few *crashes* and *bangs* within the ship interrupted her, reminding us that it would all be at the bottom of the ocean soon. We had to keep moving.

"Anton's stateroom is down here," I said, my heart pounding. "C-22."

We tiptoed up to the door.

"There's someone in there," Bridget whispered. "I can hear Mr. Gregory talking."

c

143

"It's almost time for me to go and catch a lifeboat," I heard Anton say. "It's a shame you won't be coming along, Victoria. Unless you tell me where it is."

"I told you, I don't know!"

"Then you'll have to tell me where your thieving son went."

I threw the door open and barged in. "Right here, Gregory."

There was Mother, sitting in a chair, her face chalky white. Anton was hovering over her with a pistol.

"What are you doing here?" Anton exclaimed. "You're the one who stole the notebook! You or that weasely German. You've messed with the wrong man, the wrong people!" He rolled up his sleeve to reveal a Black Hand tattoo.

He trained the gun on me. "Where's my notebook?"

"It's already left the ship," I replied, truthfully. "Now let my mother go. She had absolutely nothing to do with it."

"Ha!" Anton snorted. "I'm so sorry, John, but I'm afraid I can't do that."

"Well, I've arranged for your notebook to be delivered to the weasely German if you don't." I was bluffing, but Anton lunged for me.

"I'll shoot you dead, you son of a bitch," he growled. "Prepare to die at the hands of Serbia!"

"No!" Mother screamed as he pressed his gun against my throat.

All of a sudden, there was an enormous *whack* against the back of Anton's head. It hit him with such force that he crumpled to the floor, gun pinned beneath him.

"Oh, God," Bridget said breathlessly, covering her mouth with her hand. She was standing behind Anton, holding the stateroom's heavy lamp post with both hands. "Did I kill him? I didn't mean to kill him. Oh God…" She started to hyperventilate.

"Calm down," I said, tapping Anton with my shoe. He wasn't moving. "You did nothing wrong, Bridget. Nothing."

Another hideous groan emanated from the lower decks. The ship sounded like a dying beast. Somewhere below us, I thought I heard the sound of rushing water.

"Let's get out of here before it floods!" I yelled.

I grabbed Mother's hand and pulled her out of the chair, which she was still frozen to in fear. We ran.

"John," Mother said, tears of relief forming in her eyes. "I was petrified of what might happen to you and Sadie."

"What happened? How did you end up here?"

"Charles tricked me into going out on the promenade with him, saying we should talk.

145

Stupidly, I believed him. I hoped maybe he reconsidered the divorce. Instead, Anton was waiting on the deck—with a gun! After everyone left for the Boat Deck, they forced me back into his stateroom."

"Well, we don't have to worry about him anymore," I replied. "Either he's dead, or he'll be resting on the ocean floor when he comes to. Good riddance."

"Where's Sadie?" Mother asked. "Please tell me she's safe."

"She's in a lifeboat with Celia," I replied. "Now we have to get you to one."

In our race for the Boat Deck, we merged with a group of third class passengers who had finally broken out of steerage. The electricity was starting to falter, sending sparks flying into the air around us. We scrambled up the Grand Staircase in semi-darkness.

"The sea is coming in!" a man carrying a little girl shouted. I looked down at the foamy water gurgling up the stairs behind us. Over the ringing in my ears, I could hear Mother gasping as she tried to keep up. I reached out for her hand.

"We're almost to the deck," I told her. "Don't give up now. Run. Please, Mother, don't give up!"

On the Boat Deck, crewmen were standing around a lifeboat with their arms locked together. Lightoller was in front of them, guarding the boat with his gun.

"Only women and children will get past us," Lightoller asserted. "Any man who tries to rush this boat will be shot on sight!"

"Go to hell!" a passenger shouted. The crewmen tackled him.

"Mother, get in!" I ordered, pushing her toward the boat. "It's your last chance."

She hugged me and kissed my forehead. "We'll see each other in the morning," she said. "I know we will. As you told me, don't give up now."

"I love you, Mother," I said, swallowing hard against the lump in my throat.

The crewmen pulled her through their man-made gate. The third class man passed his little girl through, and Mother hoisted her on to her lap.

"What about you, miss?" a sailor said, reaching out to Bridget. "Step aboard. Come on, now. Don't be afraid."

"No," she said. She stepped aside to let a group of Assyrian women and children climb aboard. "I'll stay here and take my chances with you, John."

I heard a familiar accent calling my name.

"Rudy!" I exclaimed, shocked to see him here. "I looked for you earlier today."

"I thought you would," he said. "I meant to find you, too. Did you find anything in Gregory's stateroom?"

"Yes," I said. "I found a notebook filled with secret information about the Black Hand. Faye smuggled it off the ship."

"The notebook! That's what I've been looking for this whole voyage!" Rudy cried. "I tried to get into the purser's safe and the cargo hold, to no avail. I was starting to think I received bad intelligence. I didn't know it was in his room the whole time."

He stood there frowning for a minute.

"I have to get that notebook," he finally said. "It's very dangerous for Faye to have it in her possession. I *must* secure it." His face was panic-stricken as he watched the crewmen load the last lifeboat.

"Are there any more women and children?" Officer Lightoller called out.

"Here," Bridget said to Rudy, unwrapping her shawl. "Put this on and pretend you're a lady."

"What?"

"Go ahead," Bridget said. "I have no use for it anymore."

"Last call!" Lightoller shouted.

Rudy pulled the embroidered shawl over his hair and knotted it under his neck. His gangly frame was hidden beneath a long wool coat. As long as he kept his head down, no one would be the wiser.

"One more!" I said loudly, and led him by the arm to the boat, as if I were escorting a woman. Luckily, I was a head taller than

Rudy. Lightoller didn't even take a second glance at him as he sat in the boat, eyes downcast.

"Goodbye, Mother," I said as the boat began lowering. There was only a fifteen-foot drop to the water now. She kept looking back at me, even as the sailors began rowing into the night.

The band was still playing ragtime. In the distance, I spotted Jim and his friends running toward us—no lifebelts, missing coats. They would only slow them down.

"Bridie!" Jim cried. "Why are you still here?"

He looked around, dread-filled. "The boats are all gone! That was the last one!" For a second, he looked like he might burst out crying. "Why, oh why didn't you get into a boat when you had the chance?"

The passengers still aboard were scattering, running astern. Some of them took their chances and jumped overboard. They knew they would up in the water eventually, so they might as well accept their fate and go now.

Officer Lightoller stopped the crewmen from running away.

"Come back here!" he shouted. "Let's cut this boat down!"

I looked up and saw that there was one boat, a smaller one with collapsible canvas sides, still fastened to the roof of the officer's quarters. It was our only hope...if anyone could free it.

"Bridie," Jim said, "you'll get in this one!"

For the first time, she nodded. "Yes," she breathed, watching the water lapping at the Boat Deck.

Crewmen set upon the boat, frantically trying to get it down from the roof.

"Does anyone have a knife?"

"I do, right here!" Jim yelled. He jumped, and the other men hauled him onto the officer's quarters. He pulled out his pocketknife and began sawing away at the ropes, racing against time.

A mass of steerage passengers was huddled together on the deck. "We can now prepare to meet God," a voice within the huddle spoke. The passengers murmured in response.

"Hail Mary, full of grace..."

"Oh, Father Byles," Bridget said. It was the Catholic priest I'd met a few nights ago on the deck, the one who persuaded Jim not to beat me up. Bridget wandered over to him, crying softly, and dropped to her knees. Father Byles made a sign of the cross on her forehead as she prayed.

"He refused a seat in two different lifeboats so he could save souls," a crewman next to me scoffed. "He better save them quicker. We're going under."

Jim poked his head over the side of the officer's quarters. "Conkling, come give us a hand!"

I crawled onto the roof and began working furiously, getting the tangles of ropes loose while Jim sawed at them.

On the deck below, I saw one of the firemen who had been hoarding liquor in the smoking room. He drank straight from a bottle now, stumbling around woozily.

"What are you doing? Come up here and help us with this boat!" Lightoller ordered.

"Forget it, man," the fireman replied. "There's no hope now."

Suddenly, the ship wrenched downward and trembled violently. Several of the men around me careened off of the officer's quarters. I had no time to grab them as they were swept into the ocean. A stampede of passengers surged up the Boat Deck, abandoning the boat, screaming and fleeing for safety where there was none.

"There's no time!" Lightoller said, as the collapsible boat finally crashed onto the deck. "There's water pouring into her!" The ship groaned and shuddered. I felt the sting of the icy water hit my nose.

"John!" Jim screamed as he clawed at the side of the officer's quarters.

I held onto him with all my might, trying to pull him back onto the roof.

All of a sudden, I heard a noise like an oncoming train. There was a loud, terrifying whistle coupled with a great *whoosh*. The *Titanic*'s first smokestack came crashing down, crushing the people who had been swept off the ship. It sent another wave rushing over the Boat Deck.

I lost my grip on Jim. The force of the ship sucked me underwater, completely blinding me as the *Titanic*'s lights flickered, then went out forever.

Nine

I surfaced just in time to see the second funnel collapse. The explosions coming from inside the ship were deafening, punctuated by the tearing and twisting of metal. Even in total darkness, I could see the ship start to split in two. Sparks and flames shot into the air. The people still on board looked like a swarm of bees, hovering around the stern.

The sight of it was almost enough to distract me from the cold.

I put my hand out and felt something substantial bobbing up and down in the water. A pair of strong hands grabbed my shoulders.

"Not him, he's too big!" someone said. "He'll sink us all!"

It was the collapsible boat, floating upside down. At least twenty men were clinging to it, including Officer Lightoller and the drunken fireman, who was still holding on to his bottle.

"Here," he said as I pulled myself to my knees. "Take the chill out of the air."

Lightoller grabbed the bottle and chucked it into the ocean.

"Get a grip on yourself, you drunken fool," he snapped. "We have to keep this boat upright if we intend to live."

We floated past two female figures, wet hair matted to their cheeks. I could tell from their coats that they were steerage passengers.

"Hold on to me, miss," Lightoller said. But as he pulled her from the water, her head lolled to one side, eyes were half-open.

"Nevermind," he said. "These ones are dead already."

Suddenly, the second female figure raised a hand in the air.

"Let me on," she cried weakly. "I'm hurt!"

It was too dark to see the woman's face, but she had a voice I'd know anywhere.

"Bridget!" I shouted, and reached for her, nearly flipping the boat upright. There was a gash above her left eyebrow. Blood was trickling down her face and lifebelt.

"Leave her!" a crewman barked. "She won't make it to morning. There's no room for the half-dead on here."

"For God's sake, she's a girl!" someone else responded. "Now be a man and help her aboard."

Bridget flopped onto the boat, face-down. I knelt down, being careful not to rock the boat, and propped her up in my lap. We both shivered uncontrollably.

"Bridget," I said, shaking her. "Are you alright?"

She didn't respond.

"Bridget, please answer me."

"I was washed overboard with Father Byles," she said through chattering teeth. "And I hit my head against something…" She tried to raise her hand to her forehead, but was too frozen to feel it. "Something hard."

The *Titanic*'s stern was standing at a steep angle, the propellers pointing at the heavens. It hovered there a minute, then began a steady plunge. A few clumps of desperate people still clung to the rails.

My mind flashed to all the magnificent sights on the ship. The Grand Staircase…the Café Parisien…the oak carvings and gold statues, gone.

I couldn't bear to even think about the hundreds of people who were going down with it.

I felt numb as I watched the propellers disappear below the surface of the ocean, and not just from the cold. No one aboard our overturned boat breathed a word. I turned Bridget's face away so she wouldn't have to see it.

After minutes of stunned silence, Lightoller said, "She's gone."

The wrenching sounds from within the ship were no longer drowning out the blood-chilling din of the people in the water. In every direction, there were flailing figures — wailing, praying, gasping, but still very much alive.

Lightoller bit his lip. I could see that the senior officer felt partly responsible for the horror around us, yet powerless to stop it.

"Well, don't just sit there!" he snapped. "Pull some of these people aboard as fast as you can."

We pulled aboard every frantic swimmer who managed to paddle to us, limbs nearly immobilized by the hypothermia. The upside-down collapsible was supporting a ragtag mix of crew, first class men, and steerage passengers. After twenty minutes, two of them were dead from the cold. The drunken fireman gently nudged them off the hull of the boat, letting them float away to make room for others.

"Do you see any more alive?" Lightoller asked.

"No, sir," another crewman responded, "none that we can reach. They're dying quickly."

"We have no oars," Lightoller lamented. "No oars and no light."

The overturned collapsible drifted aimlessly among the *Titanic*'s debris. I could spot the green lanterns from the other lifeboats off in the distance. I wondered if they'd ever realize we were stranded here.

If not, we were doomed.

"My brother," Bridget whispered. "He's dead, isn't he?"

Silver light from the stars illuminated the wreckage around us. The wails of the swimmers were dying down; most of them bobbed up and down in their lifebelts, motionless. I didn't dare tell her that I had seen Jim vanish underwater.

"They're all dead," Bridget continued. "Jim, and the boys, and the new friends we made, all hoping for a new life…" As I held her head in my lap, cold tears trickled down her face. She was still bleeding from the forehead.

"Don't say that," I said. "You can't give up now, Bridget. We'll be rescued in no time."

"It's true," a weak voice said. I turned to find Harold Bride, the wireless operator, clinging to the boat, his feet dangling over the sides. "There's another ship coming for us."

"How do you know?"

"I am — was — one of the wireless operators aboard," Bride said. "We started putting out the distress call at midnight. Several ships responded, they just didn't make it in time."

"There's another ship nearby," Harold Bride said, "maybe ten miles off. If you look over there, you can see her lights."

He was right. If I squinted hard enough, I could see the faint yellow lights of a steamer that was stopped somewhere in the distance.

"It's the *Californian*," Bride said. "We couldn't reach her over wireless."

Officer Lightoller looked ready to explode. "Why the hell not?" he demanded.

"Her operators kept sending us ice warnings today, over and over again," Bride said. "Finally, my partner wired back, 'Shut up, I'm busy.' Then the *Californian* went silent. I would guess that the operator is in bed for the night. A Cunard Line steamer will be here at four."

I dug out my watch. It was stopped at a little past two in the morning, when I went into the water. We still had at least another hour to wait—another agonizing hour of trying to keep the collapsible upright, of trying to keep Bridget awake. I held my finger under her nostrils to make sure she was still breathing.

"Keep talking to her," Lightoller ordered me. "Keep her conscious until the rescue ship arrives." Bridget looked disoriented, staring blankly up at the sky. I wasn't sure what to say to her.

"I shouldn't have given my shawl to your friend," she said before I could speak.

"You mean Rudy? Why not?"

"It was all I had left of my mama," Bridget replied quietly. "She made it for me. I knew it was getting ragged, but I couldn't bear to part with it. Now I have nothing. Nothing and no one."

I wasn't sure how to respond. If she lost hope now, she wouldn't survive til morning. A few more of the men—tough, sturdy crewmen—had succumbed to the cold and slipped off the boat.

"You have me," I said.

"You don't know me," Bridget replied, with more a tone of hopelessness than anger. "You don't even know my name, do you?"

"No, I don't."

The wind was beginning to pick up ever so slightly, and I started to comprehend just how cold I was. My clothes were soaked through, and the only body part that wasn't numb was my icy, stinging face. I could feel the disorientation setting in. The others must have felt it, too, because no one spoke.

Finally, Bridget said, "Burke."

"What?"

"That's my name," she replied. "If you make it and I don't, remember it. Tell anyone who asks that I held on as long as I could. And that I confessed my sins to Father Byles before we sank."

"Bridget Burke," I repeated to myself. "I'll remember."

"The Burkes were one of the tribes of Galway," Bridget said. She was rambling now, sounding like she was someplace far away. "They were a noble family, back when it mattered. All of Ireland is poor now."

"I was born in a place called Connemara," she said. "In a little house by the sea. It is the most beautiful place in all of Ireland…you'll never see anyplace so green. My daddy used to tell me I had eyes the color of Connemara stone."

I thought of how brightly Bridget's eyes had shone under the *Titanic*'s deck lights. I could still see them in the semi-darkness, even as the rest of her face turned cold and grey.

"Then he died young, like most Irish men do," she said. "That was when we went to the big city. It was brown and ugly there, but at least my mama could work. She was a sewing girl. She always hoped I'd be something better. But I'm not, am I?" She was starting to tear up again.

"No," I replied. "That's not true. You'll have a new life now. You'll never have to be somebody's maid again."

Bridget snorted. "That's easy to say when you're a Conkling."

"I told you that I'm not," I said. "I was born John Merriman. My father was a professor at Oberlin. It was my mother who came from money, but he taught me there was more to value in life."

I took a deep breath, trying to stay awake. "Then a fever swept through the campus one spring, and he was gone. Mother's insurance plan was to marry Charles two years later.

I'm sure she thought she was doing right by me," I said. "She had no idea what she was getting into."

"Sometimes, I still hear my father's voice in my head, guiding me toward the right thing to do. And it's never what Charles wants."

"Do you think Mr. Conkling made it?" Bridget asked. "The lifeboats were supposed to be for the women and babes."

"I don't know," I replied. But silently, I remembered his declaration: *As you might have guessed, I have a backup plan.*

If any man could connive his way off the ship, it was Charles. At least the thought of seeing him again was enough to heat my blood.

"John," Bridget said, trying to reach into her pocket with numb, swollen fingers. "I still have this."

She handed me the necklace.

My vision was going blurry. Somewhere on the horizon, I thought I saw lights. Was it the same lights Bride had pointed out? I was too dazed to tell. I thought I heard a whistle blowing in the distance, and maybe a voice shouting. Then, silence. I dismissed it as a hypothermia-induced delusion.

"Hey, keep that girl awake!" Lightoller ordered me again.

I looked down at Bridget, whose eyes were half-open. She wasn't shivering anymore. She started to sing to herself, a slow, sad Irish song.

"*Oh Danny boy, the pipes, the pipes are calling...from glen to glen, and down the mountainside...*"

"No, Bridget," I said, trying to shake her back to alertness. "There's a ship coming. I can see it over there. Bridget..."

But before I could wake her, I felt myself slipping from consciousness, just as the lights from the approaching ship came into view.

*   *   *

I woke up somewhere dry and warm, blankets heaped on top of my chest. My vision was still blurry.

"Where am I?" I said aloud. For a second I was sure I had died and gone to heaven.

Then, the first voice I ever knew said, "Rest, John."

It was Mother.

"Do you remember being rescued?" she asked.

I rubbed my eyes. "No, I don't."

"Officer Lowe's boat took you on in the morning. We're onboard the *Carpathia* now," Mother said. "Fifteen hundred people, gone! Only seven hundred made it into the boats."

"Mommy, is Johnny alright?" a little voice asked.

"Yes, Sadie, he's going to be fine," Mother said, with a strength in her voice I hadn't heard in years. "We're all going to be fine. We'll be home in a few days."

My heart sank as I pieced together fragmented memories from the night before. "What about Bridget?" I asked, my chest filling up with dread.

Mother's face sagged. "I don't know, John," she said. "If she was rescued, she'd be downstairs with the other steerage passengers. They've turned the dining room into a makeshift hospital."

"What do you mean, *if* she was rescued?" I cried. "She was with me all night!"

"John…"

I thought of the lifeless crewmen who had been nudged off our boat, left to drift out to sea. If that had happened to Bridget…

"I'll be back," I said, as I threw on the clothes that were laid out for me. Wherever she was, I had to find her.

*   *   *

The *Carpathia*'s dining room was cramped with cots. Steerage passengers from the *Titanic* milled about, some looking relieved, others looking lost. Some hunched in the corners and wept in silence.

I spotted Mary perched on the foot of a cot and rushed to her.

"Not now, John," she said, pressing her finger to her lips. "She needs to rest."

163

Bridget was lying on her back with her eyes closed, her dark hair fanned out on the pillow. The gash on her forehead was bandaged.

"Jim didn't make it," Bridget whispered miserably.

"He is with God now," Mary replied, refusing to cry. "All the boys are."

"And I'm alone," Bridget said. "Where do I go now?"

Just then, a man in a Cunard uniform approached me.

"I beg your pardon, sir, but are you John Conkling?" he asked.

"Yes, that's me."

"First of all, my condolences for your father's demise," he said.

"What?" I exclaimed. "How do you know?"

"We pulled his body aboard today, sir," the man said. "There were several personal effects in his pockets."

I was too stunned to respond.

"I'm so sorry," he stammered. "I assumed you'd already heard the news."

"It's quite alright," I replied.

He produced a piece of paper from his pocket. "Anyway, sir, we received a telegram from his assistant in Cleveland. He said that as his heir, you alone can claim the items found with the body."

Charles didn't have time to cut me out of his will after all. Overnight, I had inherited his steel fortune. It was mine now, and I could do what I wished with it—for good or for evil.

Although Charles surely wouldn't approve, I made a vow to choose good.

"Bridget," I said, "I know where you can go."

She opened her eyes. "Where?"

"You can go to Cleveland with me," I said. "I live in a big house, not far from the lakeshore…"

"I'm sure Mrs. Conkling already has a maid," Bridget interrupted, still looking despondent. "She has no use for me."

"I don't want you as a maid."

She gazed up at me. Her eyes were red and tear-stained, but slowly, they showed a glint of a smile.

"Tell me about the big house," she said, closing her eyes again. "I want to imagine what it will be like before I get there."

I talked about Euclid Avenue and the flower garden and the beach in the summertime. I talked about Oberlin, and how she could take the carriage to visit me. I talked all night about what our new life together would be like, until Bridget at last drifted off to sleep…on a quiet sea of dreams.

Acknowledgements

When I was in the fifth grade, I became enchanted with all things *Titanic*. My first *Titanic*-themed novel was completed in the summer of 1997, at the ripe old age of 11. ("Before the movie!" as my dad pointed out in his father of the bride speech at my wedding.) That same summer, I discovered a computer game called *Titanic: Adventure Out Of Time*, by a software company called Cyberflix.

I've never grown tired of that game. So when I began this novel, I couldn't help revisiting it. Some characters and themes in this novel were inspired by characters and subplots of the computer game.

Although the game has not been sold since 2001, it still enjoys a loyal fanbase online. I would like to thank Cyberflix founder Bill Appleton for graciously giving me permission to be inspired by *Titanic: Adventure Out of Time*.

Full writing credits for the game can be found on the Internet Movie Database at http://www.imdb.com/title/tt0176236/.

Made in the USA
Charleston, SC
13 November 2013